FOREST

JANET TAYLOR LISLE

author of the Newbery Honor Book *Afternoon of the Elves*

PUFFIN BOOKS

PUFFIN BOOKS
Published by the Penguin Group
Penguin Putnam Books for Young Readers,
345 Hudson Street, New York, New York 10014, U.S.A.
Penguin Books Ltd, 27 Wrights Lane, London W8 5TZ, England
Penguin Books Australia Ltd, Ringwood, Victoria, Australia
Penguin Books Canada Ltd, 10 Alcorn Avenue, Toronto, Ontario, Canada M4V 3B2
Penguin Books (N.Z.) Ltd, 182-190 Wairau Road, Auckland 10, New Zealand

Penguin Books Ltd, Registered Offices: Harmondsworth, Middlesex, England

First published in the United States of America by Orchard Books, 1993
Published by Puffin Books,
a division of Penguin Putnam Books for Young Readers, 2001

1 3 5 7 9 10 8 6 4 2

LIBRARY OF CONGRESS CATALOGING-IN-PUBLICATION DATA
Lisle, Janet Taylor.
Forest / Janet Taylor Lisle.
p. cm.
Summary: When twelve-year-old Amber accidentally triggers a war between humans
and a community of squirrels, she finds out how similar the two species can be.
ISBN 0-14-131095-2
[1. Squirrels—Fiction. 2. War—Fiction. 3. Prejudices—Fiction. 4. Brothers and sis-
ters—Fiction. 5. Dictators—Fiction.] I. Title.
PZ7.L6912 Fo 2001 [Fic]—dc21 00-062660

Printed in the United States of America

Squirrel language

With their greetings finished, the three squirrels gathered close together, or as close as was possible with one barred away from the others. A strange series of noises, half chirp, half mew, rose out of their huddle, and it became clear that a conference of some sort was under way. What was being discussed the children couldn't tell. Nor were they prepared for the next moment, when all three squirrels turned as one and fixed them with powerful, dark eyes. . . .

◆"Beautifully crafted language. . . . A deftly plotted fantasy." —*Kirkus Reviews,* pointer review

★"In the tradition of E. B. White and George Selden, the author spins a fanciful animal yarn . . . sure to hold its audience's attention."
—*Publishers Weekly,* starred review

FOREST

·UPPER·FOREST·

The invasion occurred just before sunrise while everyone was still asleep. There was a faint rustle, the smallest scrape. Then up through branches the alien climbed, stealthy as a hunting cat. Only her eyes, those huge glistening saucers, showed in the dark.

This, at any rate, was how the inhabitants of Upper Forest later imagined her coming, for no one actually saw it happen. The Elders had posted no guards that summer night, nor had they felt a need to for some months. Cat scares had fallen off. The world had seemed at peace.

The alien was not a cat, though she came, like those murderous creatures, from below. By the time Upper Foresters awoke, she had perched herself high in the boughs of a large white oak that happened to be a hub tree in the town's branchway system. There was no missing her there. She stood out like a bear in a berry patch.

"But how did she get up?" whispered Woodbine to an uneasy crowd of squirrels gathering nearby.

"Some rope trick, probably," replied Brown Nut, his sister, jumping forward to sit beside him. "Don't look now: she's staring straight at us."

They were mink-tailed squirrels, descendants of a rugged and sharp-witted band that had settled the forest in earliest times. Now they were among its most numerous inhabitants, with wide influence over the trees in every direction.

"You know, I've never seen one of them so close up before, have you?" Brown Nut asked. "This particular alien is quite young, I think. No ears, and most of her snout is missing. Poor thing. I suppose it comes from living down there in all that dust."

"I suppose so," Woodbine answered. He took a small step forward to get a better view.

"Watch out!" cried his sister, who was older and always trying to look after him. "She might be dangerous!"

Woodbine leapt back quickly.

The town of Forest was divided into two parts, an upper part and a lower. Though they were separated by only a few dozen feet, the parts might just as well have been on different planets, so little did they have in common.

Lower Forest stretched out along the ground, as human settlements usually do. There were the usual box-frame houses set in the usual square yards, with hedges along the borders and sidewalks and paved streets out front.

Side by side, the yards spread from the big apple farms on the north of Forest to the Random River on the east and south. Edge to edge they went up Goodspeed Hill and down. There was a food store on the corner of Whipple and Whomp streets.

There was Wilbur's Pond, and the firehouse, and the musty-smelling library, and the school. Above all—and also around and among all—there were the trees. For Forest had once been a great hardwood forest, and though its trees had dwindled in recent years, many grand old groves still remained.

It was high in the tops of these, green and shadowy, that Upper Forest flourished, connected by such a complicated spiral of roadways—or branchways, as the mink-tails called the ancient limbs—that anyone looking up from Lower Forest grew dizzy and confused and soon looked away. And since Upper Foresters were just as bewildered by Lower Forest's land—so impossibly square! so ridiculously flat!—they did not very often bother to look down. The result was that there had been almost no contact between the two Forests over the years, and strangely little was known by either world about the other.

How amazing, then, to find one of the huge Lower Foresters suddenly risen up (even if she was only a youngster) into Upper Forest's leafy world. Everyone came out to stare. And to whisper:

"So ugly!"

"So awkward!"

"So noisy!"

It was true. The invader was breathing loudly, and with rude gasps. Furthermore, she was not sitting still on her branch as every young squirrel is taught to do in moments of doubt. She was leaning backward and forward, swinging her legs, turning her head. Woodbine looked on in astonishment.

"If she is not careful, she will take a tumble," remarked

Laurel, a small, graceful squirrel who was Brown Nut's friend. "I don't believe she has the least idea where she has come. She does not even have a tail."

A chucking noise erupted from several of the mink-tails. To be tailless was a great handicap in Upper Forest, a sure sign that life would be short. Some parents pushed their tailless newborns from the nest at the first opportunity. Why prolong the agony? they said.

At this moment the invader hiked forward on her branch, wrapped long, sticky fingers around the white oak's trunk, and attempted to rise on her back legs. Well, she did rise! The crowd of squirrels scrambled back.

"She is going to climb higher!" cried Woodbine. "Has anyone told the Elders what's going on here?"

"Don't worry, my dear boy. I sent for them personally," a large squirrel named Barker replied with a sniff. "They are on their way. But even the Elders' far gaze will be baffled by this. I can't recall a single story, not the wisp of a memory, of foreign trespass from below. In other times and places, yes, where trees were short-trunked. But here in Forest? It could never be done."

"Well, it has been done now, or this invader would not be here," Woodbine remarked, rather more sharply than he intended. Barker had a way of announcing his opinions, as if they were more important than anyone else's. He was one of those squirrels who like to put themselves in charge and order others around. Woodbine's ear flicked in irritation.

"Here come the Elders now, so we shall soon find out," Brown Nut declared.

Woodbine glanced over his shoulder and there they were,

just emerging from the shadows along a broad arm of the oak. Their familiar, gray-coated group moved carefully and slowly, as if, at their immense age, the Elders must pool what was left of their strength and balance to get about. And perhaps it was so, though this was not the main reason for their unity. The Elders not only traveled as one, but also spoke, gestured, slept, and meditated as one. In this way their experience was combined to achieve the greatest, the most far-reaching knowledge possible. They were a walking stockpile of memory and wisdom, the most powerful body in Upper Forest's squirrel world.

Now, as Woodbine, Brown Nut, and Laurel watched, the Elders' formation came to a halt, and their silvery heads, male and female, turned toward the invader. Their bristle of eyes examined her for a long minute. Their noses studied her scent. Finally, with a collective clearing of throats, they announced their opinion.

The invader was a girl alien from the Lower Region. ("Well, we already knew that," Woodbine muttered to Brown Nut under his breath. "Do the Elders think we are a pack of mindless beetles?")

The invader was not dangerous. She carried no weapons and seemed unlikely to interfere with their routines. She was young. She had come to their town by unknown means for a youngster's adventure. The Elders had not seen, but they had heard of, such visits before. (Woodbine glanced smugly at Barker.) In fact, a fair number of squirrel kits had dipped their paws into adventure of this sort—on the ground. There was no meaning in it. Soon the young adventurer would grow bored and go away. . . .

The Elders' speech was interrupted by a scrabbling noise. It came from the invader, who had suddenly lost her footing! With a terrific thrashing of hind legs—Woodbine's heart thumped in fright—she managed to find her branch. Shakily, she balanced upon it again.

. . . Unless she should simply fall, the Elders went on, calmly, which would save them time and trouble. However she went, she must not return. To make sure, a special troop of guards would be appointed. Its job would be to encourage the invader to leave, and when she did, to discover how she had come. Once her route was found (the Elders' decrepit tails twitched with uncanny precision), the guards could destroy it, blocking the way against future invasions.

"And May Spring Follow Winter as Day Follows Dark," the Elders intoned, to show that their remarks were ended. It was the benediction, the prayer most sacred to the mink-tailed squirrels. Many in the trees bowed their heads. Afterward the Elders gathered themselves and began to move off, their silvery raft of bodies melting slowly into the boughs' gloom.

The moment they were gone, a great clamor of chucking and chattering arose from the mink-tails, and the branches around the white oak swirled with excitement.

"You see, young fur ball," said Barker, sidling over to Woodbine. "I was right."

"Right!" Woodbine glared at him. Fur ball indeed. He and Barker were exactly the same age.

"Yes, right. The Elders did just as I said they would."

"But you never said they would do anything. You said they would be baffled!"

"You should listen more carefully. I went on to say that they would decide on exactly the course they did." Barker's voice took on a slippery tone.

"You did not!" Woodbine shouted. "You—you—liar!"

"Really, Woodbine. You mustn't allow yourself to get so excited. These childish insults . . ."

"Why, you . . . !"

"Woodbine!" Brown Nut grabbed him by his scruff in the nick of time. With Laurel's help, she dragged him away, up the white oak's trunk.

"Good grief! I thought you were going to bite him."

"Well, I would have in another second!"

"Don't let Barker tie you up in such knots. He is a cool operator and has his eye on a position on the Elders' advisory council. Stay away from him if he upsets you."

"He doesn't upset me in the least," Woodbine shouted over his shoulder. "The rat-tailed fraud!"

By now the invader had climbed to a place some twenty feet higher in the white oak. Woodbine caught sight of her snoutless face peering through the leaves. Despite their mink-tail racket, she was not looking at them. She was staring out into the distance, studying the land of her own Lower Region. And how strange it must look to her, Woodbine thought suddenly. She who had lived her whole life down there was now seeing her world from a completely different viewpoint. Woodbine leaned forward to look for himself. He was in the middle of trying to imagine how she saw things, and what life might be like in such a low-down place, when:

"Woodbine! Pay attention! You're about to fall off!" Brown Nut squawked in his ear. He caught hold of a branch just in time and swung himself back to safety. Sometimes he rather frightened himself. His mind had the strangest way of wandering off without him.

Brown Nut and Laurel had been frightened, too.

"What is wrong with you?" they chittered at him together. "Picking fights, mooning around on branches!"

"And you never do any work," Laurel told him severely.

"Everyone is worried about you, not just us," Brown Nut added.

"They say you'll never last through the winter if you don't snap to and start taking responsibility," Laurel went on.

"You can start right now," Brown Nut urged. "The Elders have gone back to Great Stump to choose the alien's guards. We are going to see if we can make the troop!"

"Come on!" cried Laurel.

They were off in a flash of tails, flicking down limbs, along twigs, around the bends of trunks, and up the broad arcs of larger branches. Woodbine watched them for a moment. Then he turned his back and looked in another direction.

He was the sort of squirrel who did not like to join in, who would rather be alone than travel with the crowd. How could anyone think in all that chatter and confusion? He did not like to wrangle with the other mink-tails for the nuts or nests or territory always under dispute. Quietly he stood aside and took whatever was left over. Or he simply went away to another place.

"You are headed for the compost pile!" his father fumed. "How do you expect to get along in this world?"

There was no answer to that. Woodbine would shrug uncomfortably and look away. The truth was that he was interested in other things: in distant views, for instance, and lower worlds. And now this invader. For some reason, Woodbine could not keep his eyes off her. No sooner had Brown Nut left than he began, cautiously, to creep closer.

The girl alien had stopped panting and was sitting astride a branch. One arm was thrown around the white oak's trunk. Her face was still turned toward the ground, but Woodbine saw that she was not really looking there anymore. She was lost in thought. Only an occasional blink, a throb of pulse on the inside of her wrist showed that she was alive. Woodbine's quick eyes took in each detail.

He climbed again and maneuvered closer. The other squirrels had gone for the moment. Most hoped, like Brown Nut, to be picked as guards, and were following the Elders back to Great Stump, their ceremonial den. Soon the chosen would return, trailing a throng of unchosen hangers-on. Then the usual haranguing and harassing would begin, for mink-tails could never idly sit by and watch, especially when the object of interest was an outsider. Now that the invader had been identified by the Elders, the Upper Foresters could have some fun. They would surround and tease her, chitter and laugh at her. Soon the alien would decide to go away—as well she should. This was mink-tail territory. She did not belong here.

Woodbine crept another few feet toward the invader. He was very close now, close enough to see the fine layer of hair that covered the skin of her legs and arms and the back of her neck. These aliens were not so bald and bare-fleshed as the stories said, it seemed. They had coats.

"Like ours," Woodbine chucked softly, "only thinner."

And then, as he strained to discover more about this creature who had come so boldly into their trees, an extraordinary thing happened. The invader's head turned, her face came around, and her two heavy-lidded alien eyes looked directly into his.

Woodbine's breath was knocked quite out of him at first, and he drew back in terror. Then, though he was tensed to run, he found himself unable to move. For, in the next second, a powerful beam of communication seemed to flow from the invader's eyes. What exactly it was, Woodbine could not be sure. Greetings of a sort, perhaps? A strange bubbling sound flowed out of her mouth. Or was it more—an offer of friendship? For a long astonishing moment, Woodbine stared back.

·LOWER·FOREST·

"She has run . . ." Wendell blurted out, stopping for breath in the middle. "She has run . . . she has run away!"

"Oh no, not again." Mr. Padgett opened his eyes and gazed sleepily at his son, who stood at the door of the bedroom in yellow summer pajamas. "What time is it, anyway?" he asked with a squint. The digital clock was a blurry lump on the dresser across the room.

Wendell turned to look. "Six-thirty-one. She's been gone for an hour at least. I felt her bed. It's cold."

Mrs. Padgett rolled over and lifted her head off the pillow. "What's happened?" she croaked.

"It's Amber," Mr. Padgett informed his wife. "Wendell says she's run away."

"Oh no, not again."

There was a pause while everyone tried to think of where she might have gone this time.

"Amber was angry," Wendell offered at last. "She was really mad—that's why she left."

"So what else is new?" his father said. "Amber's always mad. She's mad as a hatter at the whole human race. There's hardly been ten minutes in the entire last year when she wasn't—"

"Do you think she could have gone up over Goodspeed Hill?" Mrs. Padgett broke in. "Oh dear, I hope she hasn't gone up over that hill again. We took all day last time finding her in that ravine. Remember how she'd crawled into that cave and decided to—"

"No, she wouldn't be there," Wendell said. "She told me she'd never go back there. Snakes."

"That's a blessing."

There was another pause.

"Why was she mad this time, Wendell?" Mrs. Padgett inquired.

Wendell was Amber's eight-year-old brother. He was the only person who knew anything about her these days. Ever since she'd turned twelve, Amber had been mad.

"She said the world was a sick place," Wendell answered. He came forward and climbed into bed between his parents, who moved over to make room. "She said she was sick of living in a sick place. She wants to go someplace else."

Mr. Padgett shook his head. "A sick place. A sick place. That's what she always says. What is it supposed to mean?"

Wendell shrugged. "Amber says people have started to like killing each other. She says they like having fights. It's gotten into their blood. Every time you turn on the TV, there's somebody shooting somebody else, or there's some war somewhere with people getting blown up. She says she can hardly stand it anymore."

"That's a wonderful reason to run away at five-thirty on a

Sunday morning," Mr. Padgett said. "Just wonderful." He sat up, took his glasses from the bedside table, and put them on. "So what else?" he asked, turning a sharpened gaze on Wendell. "Did she say anything else?"

"That's all."

Mrs. Padgett sighed.

"She said she knows it's going to happen here, too," Wendell said. "Sometime."

"*What* will happen?" asked his parents together.

"A war," Wendell said.

Mr. Padgett snorted.

"She did. She said so," Wendell protested. "Because it's in the blood."

"Well, I'm getting up," Mr. Padgett announced. "I'm getting up and having a bowl of shredded wheat. And then I'm declaring war on the lawn. It's grown about two feet in a week. Wherever Amber has gone this time, I don't care. She can stay there forever. I'm not wasting my Sunday tramping all over town looking for her. She has some strange idea in her head again, that's what it is. She reads some book or sees something on television, and the next thing you know, she's off on the warpath, furious because nobody can understand How She Feels. Well, I've had it, let me say. This is the last time I—"

"Wait a minute, Leonard." Mrs. Padgett held up her hand. "Just hold on one minute. Did you and Amber happen to have a . . . um . . . conversation about something recently?"

"A conversation is hardly what I would call it."

"Leonard! For heaven's sake. What did you say to her? When was this, last night?"

"Nothing!" bellowed Mr. Padgett, throwing back the covers. He leapt out of bed. "I didn't say anything. She was the one who was yelling. About guns and missiles, some TV program she'd seen. Why do they put that sort of stuff on the air? I told her not to get so excited. She's just a child. How can she understand what's happening out in the world? Our government has specialists who study these things. They know what they're doing when they send our army in to—"

The bathroom door slammed, cutting off his voice.

Mrs. Padgett had also risen by this time. Wendell now occupied the bed by himself. The extreme wideness and emptiness of the sheets gave him a delicious feeling. It was a feeling of freedom and, at the same time, of perfect safety. He stretched his legs far down under the blankets and flung out his arms.

"Look at me! Look at me!" he cried to his parents. Mrs. Padgett turned around to look. Mr. Padgett opened the bathroom door.

"I'm in a giant swimming pool!" shrieked Wendell. "I'm floating around in this giant pool. I'm swimming, and now I'm . . . going . . . to . . . *dive!*"

Wendell stood up and plunged headfirst under the covers, uprooting the blankets on every side. There came the unnerving sound of a sheet ripping.

Mr. Padgett shot a furious glance at his wife. "Kids! There are times when I could just . . ." His hands seemed to grope for an invisible neck. "Yes, I do believe I really . . . could . . . just . . ."

A sudden burst of rustling and chattering erupted from the trees beyond the bedroom window, and his voice trailed off.

"What is that? Squirrels?" Mrs. Padgett asked brightly. She raised the shade to peer outside.

Much as Mr. Padgett had sworn and declared that he did not care where his daughter had gone, or whether she ever came back, twenty minutes later he was standing on the sidewalk in front of his own house, looking anxiously up and down the street. Beside him stood Wendell, eating a piece of buttered toast.

"You know you said more to her than that, Dad," Wendell said with a full mouth.

"I did not."

"You did too. Remember after you stopped yelling at her about the government—"

"I was not yelling," Mr. Padgett said.

"Well, after that, anyway, remember how she started talking about that mass murder down in Texas?"

"What mass murder?"

"You know, when that man came in a restaurant with a machine gun and just started mowing people—"

"Wendell! What kind of talk is that?"

"And there were heads busting open and eyeballs popping out and blood pouring everywhere, and some fat old lady got shot in the—"

"Wendell! Will you be quiet!"

"It wasn't where you think, Dad," Wendell said in a hurt voice. "It was just in the—"

"*Wendell!* What is wrong with you? The whole neighborhood can probably hear."

Mr. Padgett looked around in alarm. Luckily, there was no one nearby, just another bunch of squirrels chasing each other in the trees overhead. He lowered his voice. "And anyway, you shouldn't be listening to stuff like that."

"Right," said Wendell, taking another bite of toast. "That's exactly what you told Amber. Eggs-zackly. And then you smacked her."

"I did not."

"Yes you did."

"Well, she wouldn't listen!" his father cried. "What else could I do? Amber won't listen to anyone anymore. All she does is watch a lot of hogwash on TV that gives her a crazy view of the world. It's given you a crazy view, too. People don't normally go around shooting each other, you know. Not educated people. Not civilized people, like us. For instance—"

"Amber says there's no such thing as civilized people," Wendell cut in. "She says—"

"Will you stop interrupting?" Mr. Padgett interrupted. He put his hands on his hips and glared at his son. "As I was saying: for instance, here in Forest there's never been one shoot-out. There hasn't been a single murder, and no bomb has fallen or ever will. This is a safe town. What I was telling Amber was, she doesn't need to worry. The only way someone could get shot here is if some maniac came in from outside. And the chances of that happening are about a zillion to one. . . . Come on," he said, after another look up the street. "Let's start walking around and see if anybody noticed her leaving this morning."

"They didn't," Wendell said, trailing his father warily down the sidewalk. "No one sees Amber when she doesn't want them to. She's smart. She knows how to get around. She's got ways of seeing and knowing that you wouldn't believe. Someday she's going to be president of the United States. She even told me."

Mr. Padgett wheezed. "That's just the kind of thing Amber would say. Give her an inch and she'll take a mile. . . . What on earth is going on with the squirrels around here?" he added as another terrific rattling of branches sounded overhead. "Whenever I look up, there's a big rat pack of them running through the trees. Maybe it's time to get out the old shotgun and cut back the number a bit. How about it, Wendell? Have you ever been squirrel hunting?"

·UPPER·FOREST·

Screeches, jeers, and cackles echoed along Forest's limb avenues. A flock of wood sparrows perching nearby in a hickory tree flushed upward. Woodbine's ears flattened against his head. With a last glance at the invader, whose attention had turned once again to the ground, he scampered away.

The guard troop was returning, running with such eagerness that the branches rattled under their feet. Clearly, the Elders had completed their troop selection. As the first guards streaked by, Woodbine crouched in the rotted hollow of a trunk, wishing he might somehow warn her, that curious, snub-faced creature, not to be frightened. This ragtag band would never dare to touch her.

"You'll be all right! Keep a tight grip and climb down slowly," he would have advised her, if only she could have understood. "We mink-tails are a bunch of soft apples at heart. We'd never do anything to really hurt anyone."

He caught a glimpse of Brown Nut and Laurel springing past with the others. Whether they had been chosen as official guards, he couldn't tell. They disappeared up through leaves in the direction of the invader.

The teasing soon began, so loud and shrill that Woodbine fled. He did not want to watch. He took himself away to a pleasant grove of maples that grew around the eastern edge of Forest's only pond. There, with a few wary flicks of his tail, he descended into the prickly heart of a blackberry bush for a meal.

Afterward, still feeling queasy from the morning's excitement, he curled up in the crook of a tree root and fell asleep. He didn't wake until midafternoon, when a twig snapped close by.

He was up the nearest maple in a second, circling the trunk expertly to confuse the enemy. Reaching the first limb, he turned about and looked down. Directly below him, a large golden-haired canine passed within inches of the blackberry bush. It paused to sniff and lift a leg, then loped on. Woodbine watched, frozen against the branch.

He had barely recovered from this shock when he spotted a second dog. It was one of the fierce black retriever hounds that were a constant threat to fallen or disabled mink-tails. Across the field, it snuffed along a hedge of overgrown vines.

A third dog appeared from behind the hedge. And then in the distance, baying self-importantly, a fourth galloped out. This was unusual. For the first time, Woodbine realized that something was amiss in the hazy world beneath him. With extreme caution, he climbed higher up, keeping the tree's trunk between himself and the dogs. It was unlikely that they would spot him, canine eyes being notoriously dim, but he was not one to take risks.

He had no sooner settled into his new perch than an even more extraordinary sight appeared. A group of aliens came into view, walking slowly across the field near the pond's western bank. To the south, he saw other aliens striding along the edge of the woods. And others, in other unusual places: climbing over stone walls, pushing through brush. Shouts, whistles, and yelps sounded from all directions in the hot, still late-summer air. Woodbine crouched, rigid as bark, against the bark of the maple.

The Lower Region was hunting for something. The ground was being examined, the bushes probed. As the sun began to set, and evening's purple tide of shadows rose slowly up the trees, the noise of the hunt seemed to increase, and the cries and tramping below grew more frantic. Only when the light began seriously to fail did the aliens stop their search. They huddled in the middle of a field, bubbled and muttered for a while, and left the place together. A final flurry of whoops and cries echoed back before the air around the pond grew silent again. Then slowly, uneasily, the fields and surrounding woods relaxed, and the usual evening cycles took hold once more.

Woodbine sat up on his branch and looked about. He was still shaking a bit. The dogs in particular had unnerved him. He was not altogether sure they wouldn't spring out again, though he knew them to be adoring slaves of the aliens. And the aliens were not looking for him. They had not even known he was there. They were searching for the invader, of course. Woodbine had guessed it in the first moments.

She must, he supposed, still be hanging on up in the white oak—hiding out, it seemed now. Everyone for miles around had heard the hunters' wails. She must have heard them, too. But why was she hiding? Woodbine could not see into her strange alien mind. Perhaps she had not invaded their trees so much as fled from her own flat world? In which case, she should be treated as a guest, not teased and hounded like an intruder. But was this true? Woodbine was unsure. He did not like to question the Elders, who were nearly always right in matters of this sort.

Darkness had now fallen over the field. With a series of leaps, Woodbine struck out for home. At times, feeling night at his heels, he made use of a telephone wire that stretched across an open place, or an alien's roof when it offered a short-cut. But mostly he kept to trees whose paths he knew and trusted. For some strange thing was brewing in Forest. He felt it rising in waves from the ground, reaching up through the trees. Some balance had been upset. A queer smell rode the wind. Whether this had to do with the invader, or the aliens at the pond, or an event yet to be, Woodbine did not like it. Something was coming. No, it wasn't good.

He was just passing through a beech tree, heading toward the hollow tulip tree that was home nest to his family, when a flash of white underbelly caught his eye.

"Woodbine! Wait." His sister leapt through the leafy dark and skittered up beside him.

"Where have you been all day?" she chucked furiously. "Do you know what's happened? The Elders are in a rage."

"I've been out by the pond," he replied. "Something has gone wrong in the Lower Region. The hairless ones are tramping about in groups. Their canines are stalking un-leashed through the fields."

"That's just it! They are looking for the invader. She's still here!" Brown Nut cried. "Up the big white oak. Nothing we did could make her move an inch."

"I thought so!"

"We screamed ourselves hoarse and even threw seeds. Laurel and I were both chosen as guards . . . on the morning shift, no less. The alien would not leave. In fact, she hardly seemed bothered. In the middle of everything, she started to eat."

"To eat!" Woodbine gazed at his sister. Eating was something a mink-tail did only in strictest privacy and safety. No mink-tail would dare to eat during an assault of the sort the alien had gone through that day. It was unthinkable.

"She has come supplied with food. And water," Brown Nut informed him darkly. "They're stowed in a pouch on her back. Many believe it is a sign of her bad intentions. A rumor is about that she has come to drive us away, or, at the least, to take over the town."

"But why?" cried Woodbine, now even more appalled. "She can't even climb. Why would she want to live here?"

"No one knows, and that is part of the problem," Brown Nut replied. "No one understands why she should have come to begin with. And no one understands why she refuses to leave. No one knows what is in her mind, or what her plan may be. This leads to guessing, and guessing leads to imagining, and imagining leads to fear. Meanwhile, the Elders hold endless councils and mutter into their tails."

"Listen. This invader is nothing to be afraid of," Woodbine said. "I went up quite close to her. There was only friendship in her eyes, which were powerful but very open. She is more in danger of us than we of her, I should say. It's amazing she hasn't fallen already with all your hounding."

"Try telling that to the Elders. They have charged her with

official trespassing, now, and ruled her highly dangerous to the town."

"Highly dangerous! But that's ridiculous. What has gotten into the Elders?"

"Whatever it is, the invader will spend the night here, I suppose," Brown Nut said. "Under heavy guard. Then the problem will be taken up again in the morning. Meanwhile, I'm heading home. It's way past time for us to be inside. Look, here's the moon."

It had been rising slowly all during their conversation. Now, suddenly, the moon sprang into view, pouring a shimmering light upon the leaves and boughs around them.

"How beautiful. Beautiful!" Woodbine cried in spite of himself. "It's as big as a pond tonight. No—as big as a . . ." He paused to think. "As big as an ocean!"

Brown Nut sighed. "As if you knew how big an ocean was. As if you've ever set eyes on one."

"Well, I can imagine," Woodbine said. "The old stories have spoken of such a thing. It is quite clear in my head. And who knows, we may see an ocean one day. Who says we have to spend all our lives in this place?"

"And that, dear brother, is the whole problem with you," Brown Nut replied severely. "Who among us has time to think about distant places, much less travel to them? A little less imagining and a lot more foraging will serve us all better in the long run. The home nest, for instance, is in desperate need of repair before winter, not to mention the seed storehouse, which is still quite low, and . . ."

Woodbine was not listening. His eyes had taken on the fogged-in look that so infuriated his sister. His body sagged dangerously off the branch. No doubt he was on a beach at that very moment, gazing out at some mysterious sea.

"You're impossible. Impossible!" Brown Nut snapped at him. "You take no responsibility at all. If Mother asks where you are, I shall say you've been eaten by a cat! It's bound to come true before very much longer." She turned and headed for home.

The mention of cats brought Woodbine back to himself rather quickly. For several minutes he glanced around with nervous eyes. But then, as there seemed to be nothing moving anywhere, and as the moon was shining so brightly, he thought he might risk staying out a bit later and go to take another look at the invader. She would be under surveillance, of course. The night shift would be in charge. He made his way warily toward the white oak, avoiding guards. Most of them were dozing at their posts.

The invader was not asleep. Her enormous eyes glistened in the moonlight. Her fingers were busy moving here and there. She rustled about on her high branch, taking things from a pouch, putting other things back. At one point she grasped an odd, long-necked instrument and proceeded to rap it loudly on the tree. The guard minks sprang up at this, but shortly, as no danger seemed to come from it, they settled themselves again. The rapping continued at intervals.

Some time passed before Woodbine, hidden behind leaves several yards away, began to see what the invader was doing. Why he should have been so surprised he didn't know. It was exactly what he would have done under the circumstances. It was what any of them in Forest would do—mink-tails, crows, raccoons, possibly even cats (those slinking muggers)—after

finding themselves alone, in a strange place at night, surrounded by unfriendly natives.

"She is building a nest!" Woodbine whispered to the nearest
guard. But since this individual was sound asleep, whiskers
fluttering, he went on whispering in excitement to himself.

"How absolutely amazing and incredible! A nest!"

·LOWER·FOREST·

Mr. Padgett was worried about his daughter. Up the room he strode with hard, angry steps. Back he came, red-faced and bug-eyed.

"She's been kidnapped!" he roared. "That's what it is. She's been kidnapped by some shiftless, cowardly criminal. From the big city, most likely. That's where they come from. How he found Forest, I don't know."

"Probably looked it up on the state map!" someone yelled from the rear of the crowd. They had all—search party, dogs, children, and mothers—come back to the firehouse after nightfall put an end to the search. Now homemade sandwiches were being handed around. Warren Wilbur from the food store had brought over several cases of soda, along with a pack of napkins.

"Real nice of you, Warren," Tex Teckstar, the fire chief, told him.

"My pleasure," said Warren. "It's an emergency."

"I'd like to make a motion to remove Forest from the state

map!" Mr. Padgett shouted. "I'd like to make a motion to remove it from all maps. If they don't know we're here, the criminals won't come out. They'll skip over us and go on to someplace else."

"Hear, hear!" cried some voices in the crowd.

Fire Chief Teckstar took the opportunity to stand up. He was the highest ranking official in town. Lower Forest was small enough and quiet enough not to have a police department of its own. The town called on Randomville, upriver, when it needed enforcement—which it rarely did. Things pretty much took care of themselves most of the time.

"I'll make a statement, if I may," Chief Teckstar announced in his good-natured growl. He held up his hands to quell the noise and wiggling and scrambling in front of him. Most people were sitting on the firehouse's cement floor to eat, which wasn't all that comfortable. Wendell was hanging on to the fire pole that went up through the ceiling to the second floor. Every once in a while he'd practice whirling around it, and step on somebody's hand.

"Sit down, Wendell," Mrs. Padgett whispered.

"The statement I'd like to make is this," Chief Teckstar went on. "That we don't have a ransom note." He looked around at the crowd. "We don't have a ransom note, and without it, or a telephone threat, or some message asking for something, we don't know for sure that Amber's been kidnapped. In fact, we don't know anything about anything yet, so I'd say it's a little early to start making motions about taking Forest out of—"

"Then what should we do!" Mr. Padgett roared out. "We can't just sit here and let the criminals take over the town."

"Now, now, Lenny. Calm yourself. It hasn't come to that by any means." Chief Teckstar raised his big hands soothingly again. He'd handled some bad fires in his time.

"Let's look at the facts," he said. "First, Amber's a sharp kid. If she really is stuck somewhere, it's likely she can take care of herself, at least for a night, until we get reorganized in the morning. Second, she's taken off before. We all know that. And she's come back fine, except for causing her mother a bit of worry."

"A bit of worry . . . !" Mr. Padgett practically exploded at this. "She'd better not be kidding us this time, or I'll . . . I'll . . ." He started in on the same neck-wringing movements that he'd made in the bedroom that morning. Wendell stopped swinging to watch.

"Third," said Chief Teckstar. "Third, there's nothing else we can do tonight. It's dark. The dogs need rest. We need rest. I'd like to make a motion that we meet back here at seven tomorrow morning. Do I hear a second?"

"Seconded," muttered the crowd.

"All in favor say 'Aye.' "

"*Aye!*"

"All opposed say 'Nay.' "

There was dead silence, while Mr. Padgett looked daggers around the room.

"All right, then, see you in the morning!" cried Chief Teckstar.

At this point, everyone who could get up off the cement floor by themselves got up. Everyone else groaned and waited for help.

"Oh dear, oh dear, what shall we do now?" cried Mrs.

Padgett, groping for her purse. "We won't sleep a wink to-night. We'll be thinking about all the terrible things that might have happened to Amber. Where in the world can that child be?"

"Don't worry, Mom," Wendell said. "Amber's okay."

"But how do you know?"

"I just do," Wendell said. "Amber's mad. And when she's mad, she goes away to think."

"She does?" asked Mrs. Padgett, looking at him doubtfully.

"Don't you know anything about Amber by now?" Wendell demanded.

"I guess not," Mrs. Padgett admitted. She reached for the fire pole and pulled herself wearily to her feet. Around her, families were gathering together and, amid a great deal of shouting and confusion, moving toward the big, open fire-house doors. Outside, the night was hot and pleasant. Wherever she was, Amber wouldn't be cold.

"So where do you suppose she's gone?" Mrs. Padgett asked Wendell under cover of the chatter. Her eyes slid over to where Mr. Padgett stood, talking to Warren Wilbur and waving his arms.

"I dunno. Away."

"But where?"

"How do I know?"

"Guess."

"Somewhere back in the woods, probably. That's where I'd go if I was sick of living in this town. Dad whacked her, you know. She was pretty insulted."

"Hmm-mmm," said Mrs. Padgett, gazing at her husband.

"She took her knapsack and some gear," Wendell added.

"I guess she's planning to stay for a while. She'll come back, though. You don't have to worry."

Mrs. Padgett put her arm around her son's shoulders. "Wendell?"

"What."

"Let's not mention this to your father. I mean, about Amber probably being in the forest, and the knapsack and all. It's not the sort of thing he needs to hear right now."

"What do you think I am, some kind of beetle-brain?" Wendell asked his mother in an outraged voice. "Do you think I want to get killed?"

• ◆ •

Mrs. Padgett was right about not being able to sleep. Despite what Wendell had said, she wrestled and spun in her bed all night. And she wasn't the only one. Almost nobody in Lower Forest slept well. Whether this was because of Amber Padgett's disappearance, or the moon, which was full, or some strange disturbance in the air, there was no telling. All over town, lights flicked on at odd hours and floorboards creaked. Even Wendell, who always slept like a drunken sailor (as Mr. Padgett liked to say: he had been in the navy), was set upon by a terrifying dream about exploding light bulbs. He was forced to crawl into his parents' bed for comfort.

"Mom?"

"What."

"Move over."

"What?"

"Move over!"

"Ouch!"

"Wendell, is that you?"

"Sorry, Dad."

"You're on my . . . !"

"Sorry. Is that better?"

"No!"

No wonder that not long after, Mr. Padgett found himself downstairs in the kitchen, in his pajamas, at the insane hour of . . . what was it, anyway? He put on his glasses to look. Good grief—5:36 A.M.! His eyes felt like two volcanic craters. He opened the back door and went out on the porch to cool off.

The sun was just coming up. It was going to be a hot day. A hot Monday in August, he thought, and then remembered that he wouldn't be going to work that morning, not with Amber missing.

A guilty shiver ran down his spine. Why had he slapped her? He hadn't meant to. He didn't believe in hitting children. He had lost his temper. Wham—his hand had shot out. And now she had run away. Well, he would have done the same thing. There was no excuse for his behavior. Amber was a good kid, really. Smart as a whip. Dependable. Where could she be?

Mr. Padgett stepped down and walked around the house once, just to make sure she wasn't camped out somewhere. She liked to camp out. She'd take her sleeping bag into the field and spend the night there. In the open! She seemed to have a special feeling for natural places, for wild things. Mr. Padgett wondered why he'd never thought of buying her a tent. Even if she was a girl, she probably would have loved one.

His eyes traveled up toward the sky as he thought about

this, and there—good grief!—his heart gave a jump. About ten squirrels were sitting on a low-slung branch of the maple tree near the side hedge. They were looking straight at him. And then, turning his head, Mr. Padgett saw that more squirrels were on the porch roof, and others were congregated near the drainpipe over the bedroom window, and still others sat on the split-rail fence that separated their yard from the Wilsons' next door. They were all staring down at him, silent and still.

"Shoo! Shoo!" he cried, running into the middle of the yard and waving his hands. He made a pass at the maple. "Scram! Get out of here!" The squirrels scampered quickly out of reach, up into higher branches.

"Buzz off, you rodents. Get away from my roof!" The squirrels on the roof scattered and disappeared. A second later, the fence was vacant, too.

"What is going on around here?" Mr. Padgett panted, climbing the stairs to his bedroom. "The squirrels are taking over this town. Probably carrying all kinds of diseases. Rabies. Lyme ticks.

"Wendell!" he whispered into his sleeping son's ear. "Get up! We're going squirrel hunting. Now!"

"What?"

"Now! Get up!"

They were out the back door ten minutes later, Wendell still in his pajama top. He'd got his jeans on, but without the belt.

"Shush!" His father held up a hand. "Look!" He pointed into the yard.

"I don't see anything," Wendell said sleepily.

Mr. Padgett paused. "Well, that's because I scared them off. They're gone now. There were hundreds of squirrels out here. I'm not kidding! They were all watching me, as if I'd done something and they were out for revenge. I just about jumped out of my skin!"

Wendell sat down on the porch step and propped up his head on a hand. "Dad! Have you gone crazy? Squirrels wouldn't do that."

"Come on!" cried Mr. Padgett, without listening. "You can't sit down! We're going to bag us some squirrels. I've got my gun. Let's go."

"This is ridiculous," Wendell muttered under his breath as they climbed the back fence and set off toward the denser woods behind the house. Without a belt, his jeans kept sliding down, and his father was acting strange. He was walking under the trees with weird springing steps, casting his eyes right and left, like a criminal on the loose.

"Dad! What are you doing?"

"Shush!" Mr. Padgett raised his shotgun and sighted down the barrel.

"What do you see?"

"Nothing . . . yet."

They moved on, deeper into the forest. His father began to make odd crunching and clicking noises with his tongue. What these were meant to be—squirrel calls?—Wendell didn't dare ask. He would have died of embarrassment if anyone had been watching. Luckily, they were all by themselves.

"Dad. Slow down. You're practically jogging and my jeans are—"

"*Shush!* Look!"

"Where?"

"There's a whole bunch of them up in that tree."

Wendell shaded his eyes and looked up.

"Stand back!" whispered his father. He raised the gun and aimed it.

"Are you sure that's squirrels?" Wendell said, still gazing up. "It doesn't look exactly like squirrels to me. It's something bright green and sort of hanging down—"

BLAM! BLAM!

A terrifying scream came from the branches above them.

There was a long, grim silence, during which two squirrels did indeed drop to the ground, one kicking wildly.

Wendell's eyes turned round as hubcaps.

Up above, a rustling noise was followed by a scrape. A face looked down through branches and leaves.

"Dad! What are you trying to do, kill me?"

"Amber?" Mr. Padgett didn't really say the name. He breathed it.

"Amber!" screamed Wendell. "Are you okay? Are you hit?"

"I'm not hit . . . I think." Amber's face disappeared for a moment. Then her sneakers were visible, quite high up, coming down toward them. She climbed to the white oak's lowest branch—which wasn't all that low—grasped a thin rope that was hanging there, and walked herself down the trunk.

"Oh, Amber!" Wendell exclaimed when she had turned around to face them. "That was so scary. I thought you were shot for sure. Dad was aiming right at you."

"No I wasn't," Mr. Padgett protested, but his voice still sounded as if the wind had been knocked out of him. He sat down suddenly on the ground, just where he'd been standing.

"I saw some squirrels," he murmured. "I shot at them, to the left of . . ." He looked at Amber. "What is all that stuff up there?"

"It's my sleeping bag," Amber replied. "I nailed it between the branches and the trunk to make a hammock."

Mr. Padgett covered his face with both hands and shook his head slowly. "I won't ask why," he said, muffled behind his hands. "I won't. I won't."

"You can ask if you want to," Amber said. "I needed some space to think. And a little peace and quiet. I guess I almost found it. Permanently."

She glanced at Wendell and grinned, then leaned over and gave her brother a hug. He was still quite pale and wide-eyed.

"Look, Wendell." Amber squatted down. "There's a squirrel right here at your feet. It's breathing, too. Maybe it's in shock. It doesn't seem wounded."

"Maybe it fell when the gun went off, and got the wind knocked out of it," Wendell said, stretching out his hand.

"Maybe. Let's take it home. That is, if home hasn't been blasted off the face of the earth by now." Amber grinned at Wendell again. She was trying to cheer him up. They both glanced over at the hunched-up shape of their father.

"Well, it was still there the last time I looked," Wendell managed to say bravely, but his voice wobbled a bit and gave him away.

·UPPER·FOREST·

The explosion that rocked Upper Forest as the sun came up over the trees that morning frightened the town to its core. The big, black crows froze on their perches, the woodpeckers halted mid-peck, foxes and raccoons cringed upon the ground, and flies, bees, mosquitoes, and mites drained from the air. Even the little breezes that rustled constantly down Forest's broad limb avenues stood still, and the whole wood seemed to hold its breath.

Woodbine woke with a start and lay motionless in the tulip-tree den. He was alone. Everyone else was up and away, Brown Nut to morning guard duty, the rest of the family to foraging. Outside, the forest's silence was eerie and unnatural, and Woodbine's first thought was that the slow-rising evil he had sensed the day before had sprouted black wings and arrived.

But then the wood began its little rushes and squeaks again. A blue jay laughed rudely, a catbird meowed, and Woodbine poked his head out of the den. A chorus of squirrel voices was coming from the direction of the alien's oak tree. He climbed out and went to investigate, reaching the place just in time to see an angry crowd of mink-tails setting off together through the trees. Everyone was shrieking loudly.

"What is it?" he called to an old mink-tail at the edge of the throng. "Where is everyone going?"

"The invader has killed a guard!" the fellow barked back. He looked a little rattled. "A terrible explosion went off in her tree. I was right here and saw it all. Do you know the mink-tail called Woodwind? He was blown to shreds in a single instant. Many other guards are wounded. And that's not all."

The old squirrel launched himself shakily from a branch and jumped to a perch nearer Woodbine.

"One of the fallen guards has been kidnapped."

"Kidnapped! By whom?"

"The invader! It is all the work of the invader! And now other aliens have joined her. Many believe that the Elders were wrong to treat her so casually. They smell the makings of a plot. Do you know the mink-tail called Brown Nut?"

"Brown Nut!" Woodbine's eyes bulged in alarm.

"The aliens are carrying her away as we speak, through the Lower Region to their dens."

"But how . . ."

"But we will not give up so quickly, they will see. We will follow and take her back. Come on! Let's hurry and catch up with the others. Never before, in my memory, has such an outrage been committed against the town of Forest!"

These passionate words left the old squirrel rather breathless. He wavered on the branch and might have fallen if Woodbine had not leapt to his side and supported him.

"Careful, old one."

"Let me go, let me go!" the old firebrand raged, and Woodbine dropped back. He was too anxious about his sister to insist on helping, as mink-tail etiquette normally required. He scurried up several branch levels in the white oak, passed directly over the invader's nest (it was made of some wonderful mosslike material), and set off through the forest's topmost limbs.

That the invader had killed a squirrel, and was now kidnapping his sister, Woodbine could not begin to understand. He had read her eyes. They looked odd on the outside, but inside they were as civilized as any mink-tail's. She was no murdering, hunting cat, he knew. If she had been, she could have finished her work long before dawn. All night her guards had snored at their posts. She might have caught five or ten of them for breakfast if that was her design.

Woodbine began to travel rapidly through the forest. Tree to tree he went, leaping from the slimmest fingers of branches across great chasms of air. Not once did his feet make a false connection. Never did he miss the places he jumped for. He went so far so fast that he soon overran the mink-tail mob below, and found himself in front. He came partway down a maple tree at the edge of a clearing to rest and wait for the others to catch up.

He had no sooner settled himself than a scuffling noise rose from the ground and three long-stemmed figures tramped into view.

Aliens! Woodbine stiffened and watched them come. Though it was not his habit to look directly at these creatures, he forced himself to examine them as they passed beneath him.

One was very large. One was thin and small. The last figure in the group looked rather like the invader, though all aliens were so much the same, with their hairless noses and large, wobbling eyes, that it was hard to be sure. There was no question about the ragged clump of fur this last alien carried in its naked paws.

"Oh, Brown Nut!" Woodbine's heart went out to his sister with a lunge. In horror, he watched her familiar body travel by. Brown Nut had never looked small to him before. She had always loomed large in his mind's eye. For the first time, Woodbine realized how little she really was, how vulnerable. The invader was holding her respectfully, at least. (It was the invader. He could see that now.) The alien's hands were cupped around Brown Nut, as if to shield her from further danger. The alien's walk was slow and careful. Still, not one flicker of life could Woodbine see in his sister. Brown Nut's tail hung limply to one side. Her ears had fallen back.

The other squirrels began to arrive. They joined him in the maple tree, filling its branches and those of other trees and shrubs around the clearing's edge. Soon the place bristled with squirrels and every eye was fastened on the action below.

The aliens climbed a fence and marched across another clearing. They disappeared with Brown Nut into a large ground nest on the other side. At this, a wave of outrage broke out among the squirrels. Some surged forward as if to attack the nest. Others hung back and screeched fiercely.

"Do you think she is still alive?" a voice whispered by his side. Woodbine turned to find Laurel. She had seen him through the trees and come to perch near him. From the wild look of her coat, it was evident that she had experienced some violence herself. Woodbine stared at her in fright.

"Who can say! Who can say! My sister does not look very well."

Laurel's whiskers quivered angrily. "Brown Nut's eyes were open, but they saw no light, I think. It hardly matters, anyway. No mink-tail survives long in an alien den. Killers, they are. Our most ancient tales have told us. The Elders were stupid. They should have attacked this invader the minute she was discovered. A youngster she may be, but she is crafty and dangerous."

Woodbine nodded. He could not recall such tales about the aliens, but he was young himself, just two summers in age. Was it possible that he also had been fooled by the invader? Perhaps her strange eyes masked a treacherous mind.

Woodbine turned again toward Laurel. He felt a great friendship for her suddenly, and wanted to ask if she would risk sneaking closer to the alien den with him. If they got near enough, maybe they could look inside to see what was happening. Then they could make a plan to rescue Brown Nut. Woodbine was in the middle of saying these things, and Laurel was already beginning to bend her ears, yes, when—

A tremendous explosion went off. Across the way, a branch loaded with mink-tails snapped and crashed down out of a tree. Screeches broke out among the fallen, some of whom began to writhe on the ground.

Shocking as this was, there was hardly time for Woodbine and Laurel to do more than gasp before another explosion ripped through the air.

And another, shredding leaves.

And then, while scores of mink-tails toppled to the ground, and others ran for cover, two more tree-shattering blasts smashed into the rising heat of the summer morning. The first blew Woodbine and Laurel off their perch, but not before Woodbine caught sight of something.

The biggest alien had quietly returned. It was crouched around the corner of the human nest. In front of its face it held a . . . what was that thing? Woodbine searched his mind and could not find a word. But as he fell, his sharp eyes saw fire flash from a long black snout, and his ears received the crack of yet another explosion. A streak of fire seemed to rush past his cheek. Then, for Woodbine, the world darkened and went dead.

·LOWER·FOREST·

"He's hit about five squirrels so far. There's an awful scramble going on," Wendell reported from the window, which was opened to its screen.

Behind him, Amber sat on the bed pressing her hands against her ears. Her face was pale. The two were upstairs in her bedroom. Outside in the yard, the gun went off again.

"There go two more. I don't know if they're hit, though," Wendell said. A corner of the screen had come loose at the edges. He raised the flap for a better look. "Some squirrels are getting knocked to the ground by other squirrels. They're all trying to run away. Can't you stop him? It's getting pretty bad."

"What can I do?" Amber replied in a tight voice. "Throw myself, screaming, out the window? That wouldn't stop him. Nothing will."

Another gunshot sounded from the yard, then another.

"Well, that's the last shell," Wendell said. "Unless he decides to reload."

They waited tensely for what seemed a long time.

"What's happening now?" Amber whispered.

"He's walking around looking at stuff. Now he's picking up dead squirrels. He's throwing them over the fence."

"How many?"

"Six. But there might be more."

Amber took her hands off her ears and gazed down into the cardboard box on the bed in front of her. "This squirrel's a girl," she said quietly.

Wendell glanced around. "How's she doing?"

"I don't know. She's still knocked out. But she's breathing. It's strange: her eyes are open but you can tell she can't see. If she makes it, we're not keeping her for a pet."

"How come?"

"We're taking her back where she came from."

"How come?" Wendell said again, coming over to sit on the bed. He looked at his sister with grave admiration. Amber always knew the right thing to do.

Downstairs, they heard the back door to the kitchen open and their father come in. They heard him speaking to their mother, but the words weren't clear.

"Wendell," Amber said. She moved closer to him in just the way he loved. Conspiratorily. Her eyes sought his.

"I want to tell you what happened when I was out in the forest," she said. "You won't believe it."

"What!" breathed Wendell.

"There's a whole other civilization out there," Amber said. "A whole world we could never even imagine because it's so different. The squirrels have made it. They've been there for a long time, I think. Much longer than we have. There are ancient paths through the trees, and lookout points, and gathering places. There are hundreds of squirrels, old ones and young ones. They're organized. I mean, they understand who they are. One of them came right up and stared me in the eye. He was studying me, trying to find out why I was there. We would have talked to each other if we could."

"Wow!" said Wendell.

"And listen to this!" Amber went on. "They've got this troop of silver-haired squirrels that makes all the big decisions. Like our president, you know, except there's a whole bunch of them, and they move together and talk in one voice. It's the queerest thing to see. They came to look at me, too. And then they said something in some language, kind of chittery-sounding, and the other squirrels listened and did what they said."

"What did they say to do?" Wendell asked with glowing eyes. If anyone else had told him such things, he probably would have laughed.

"Well, I think they said to try to make me leave, because pretty soon a group of squirrels came back and started badgering me—in a playful sort of way. They're peaceful animals at heart. I could see it right away. They just wanted to let me know I was trespassing on their territory."

"What did you do?"

"I talked to them, and told them how lucky they were to live in such a beautiful place. Of course, they couldn't understand me. Finally most of them went away. Everything was so quiet and green in their trees. When it got dark, the moon came and shone through the leaves. I wish I could spend every night up there."

"Wow!" said Wendell. "Nobody's ever going to believe this about the squirrels."

"That's right, they won't, so don't tell anyone," Amber ordered, her voice turning angry again. "People wouldn't understand. These are not ordinary squirrels. We're going to find out more about them. I've decided to do research."

"You mean you're going back up?"

"Right, and so are you. We need two of us. That way we'll be able to back each other up if we find something important. And we're going to keep notes."

"Oh, wow!" Wendell more or less screamed. "How did you get that idea?"

"Sh-sh!"

He clapped his hand over his mouth.

"I read a book about it," Amber whispered. "See? Here it is: *Woodland Animals and Their Habitats*, by A. B. Spark. I found it in the library. The author is a professor at the university in Randomville. He traveled to all kinds of forests, all over the world, and took notes. It's not hard. We could do it.

"But first . . . " Amber went on, even more quietly, because someone was coming upstairs. They could hear the footsteps mounting. "First we've got to make this squirrel we brought home get better. That's the most important thing. Because the other squirrels are not going to want us coming into their trees again after the terrible thing Dad did unless . . ."

"Unless we do something that shows we're friends," Wendell finished excitedly.

"Right."

"Like taking this little squirrel back to her family?"

"Exactly."

Wendell reached out and, with the lightest fingers, stroked the little squirrel's furry side. He couldn't ever remember touching anything so soft.

"What about the ones that already got shot?" he asked in a low voice.

Amber frowned. "We'll bury them. Then the squirrels will know we're on their side."

"But will they really understand? Squirrels are squirrels, you know. How can they ever—"

"Wendell! That's what I've been trying to tell you. These squirrels are different. They've got different tails and different eyes. They know what they're doing. Did you see how they followed us through the woods when we took this squirrel away? They care about each other."

At this, the door of Amber's bedroom burst open and Mrs. Padgett looked in with a smile.

"Anyone want some breakfast? What is all this whispering I hear?" she asked, in the kind of stage whisper mothers use when they know they are butting in. She came across and sat between them on Amber's bed, and looked sadly at the little squirrel. Then she told Amber that no one was angry with her this time for running away, and that she hoped it wouldn't have to happen again.

"I've spoken to your father," Mrs. Padgett added, by way of explanation. "He wants to apologize to you for losing his temper the other night. But he had to rush off to work, so he'll do it this evening at dinner. All this business with the squirrels has upset him, I think. He doesn't really like to shoot things, you know."

There was an uncomfortable moment of silence during which Amber's jaw tightened and they all stared down at the little squirrel. Wendell wondered if his father had told his mother about almost shooting Amber in the tree. It appeared he had not.

"So I guess that's that," Mrs. Padgett plowed on brightly. "Everything is cleared up. Thank goodness! Now we can all get back to normal life."

Normal life! Amber glared at Wendell.

"Um, Mom," she said. "We have some plans we have to work out and a lot of stuff to think about. This has been an upsetting morning for us, too, and we're not very hungry. No offense, but would you mind leaving now so we can talk?"

Mrs. Padgett looked somewhat startled by this, but she got right up. Wendell watched her nervously.

"Of course I don't mind," their mother said. "And I understand." She gave Amber a pat on the shoulder and ruffled Wendell's hair. "Just let me know if I can be of any help." She went out, pulling the door shut behind her.

Wendell turned awestruck eyes on his sister.

"How did you do that?" he demanded. Nobody he knew and nobody he'd heard of had ever gotten away with telling their own mother to get lost.

"She even closed the door!" Wendell exclaimed in amazement. But Amber wasn't listening. She was leaning over the box.

"Look!" she said. "I think the little squirrel is beginning to wake up."

• ◆ •

Nearly an hour later, Amber and Wendell came downstairs and, passing their mother in the kitchen entry, went out the back door into the yard.

"Everything all right?" Mrs. Padgett called, after the screen door had slammed practically on her nose. "Where is the squirrel? Still up in your room?"

She tried to sound unconcerned, but was not very successful. Wild things brought into the house always made her nervous. She remembered a crow Amber had caught one time and imprisoned in the upstairs bathroom. (The shower curtain had been clawed and pecked to pieces.) And a large turtle with a nasty smell that had tried to bite her. Or was it a tortoise? The trouble with wild things was you never knew exactly what they were or what they might do.

Amber's face appeared in the door. "Don't worry, Mom. We put the squirrel in the old hamster cage."

"Oh! Has it woken up, then?"

There was no answer. The children had already walked away into the yard. Mrs. Padgett felt a sudden need to investigate for herself.

She found the little squirrel crouched groggily in a corner of the cage, which had been home to a much loved hamster of Wendell's that had escaped into a closet two months before. Unfortunately, it had never been seen again—though sometimes, late at night, Mrs. Padgett awoke and was certain she heard pattering in the walls. In fact, there seemed to be a loud, multi-pawed scuffling at times, which had led her to wonder if Wendell's hamster had somehow met up with another hamster, and . . .

Mrs. Padgett shivered. The idea that swarms of wild hamsters might be nesting just inches away from her own pillow had given her some bad moments in the middle of the night. Thank goodness morning always came to put an end to such thoughts. Nevertheless:

"Squirrels are *much larger* than hamsters, aren't they," Mrs. Padgett couldn't help remarking as she hovered over the cage in Amber's room.

She went to the window to observe her children. They had

climbed the back fence and were wandering around in the field. Looking for arrowheads, probably. Or playing Scouts and Indians. She remembered doing these things as a child. The world had been a cozy place then. So new. So innocent. So full of wonder and fantasy. Mrs. Padgett sighed.

"Well, we all grow up soon enough," she murmured. "Real life takes over with its hardness and truth. Let children have their games and silly bits of make-believe while they can."

On the way out of Amber's room, she noticed that the captured squirrel was watching her with dark eyes. Was it her imagination, or had the creature's face taken on a strangely intelligent look? Mrs. Padgett's hand rose to her throat. She walked quickly out the door.

· ◆ ·

"Amber? Here's one," Wendell said.

She came over and looked. The body was lying in the long grass, small and gray. The eyes were closed. There was a wound under the chin. A trickle of dried blood ran down the chest. Amber stared at it.

"The thing to do is lay it under a heap of leaves in the bushes," she said finally, in such an odd voice that Wendell glanced up at her. "At least, I think that would be the most natural, squirrel way of burying it, don't you?" she added, keeping her eyes down.

"I guess so."

They picked up the body, which was already slightly stiff, and carried it to a bush growing near the fence. They tucked it down among the roots so that no one would know it was there.

"Crows and hawks like to eat dead squirrels—when they can find them," Amber said. "They peck out their eyes."

"Ugh! Look, there's another body."

"Yes."

"I don't think you're looking very hard. You're mad at Dad, right?" Wendell asked. "He didn't have to shoot a bunch of dumb squirrels who couldn't even fight back. He's a creep, right?"

"Sure I'm mad at him, but it's not that simple," Amber said. "And these squirrels aren't dumb."

Wendell found three more dead bodies. They buried them respectfully, giving each a bush of its own. The squirrels had died in different ways, wearing different faces. The eyes of one were popped wide open, surprised. It was shot in the neck. Another, with a wound in the chest, was squinting and baring its teeth. The third showed no wound but was curled up, its cute little paws covering its nose.

"Well, I'm mad at Dad," Wendell said. "I'm never going squirrel hunting with him again—even if he orders me to. He almost killed you and he never even told Mom. He never even said he was sorry."

"He was sorry," Amber said. "And scared. That's why he didn't tell her. That's why he went and shot all these other squirrels, too."

Wendell looked at her. "I don't get it," he said.

"Think of it this way. When people do dumb things, they are sorry and scared. And angry at themselves. But it isn't so great being angry at yourself. You have to live with yourself, right? So then you look around for something else to be mad at. Dad was mad at himself for almost killing me, so he took it out on these squirrels. If you asked him, I bet he'd say: They made me do it!"

"But that's crazy! He's the one who did it, all by himself."

Amber shrugged. "Who ever said human beings weren't crazy?" she asked.

A half hour more of looking produced nothing, so they called off the hunt. But on the way back to the house, they caught sight of a squirrel lying half-hidden in the grass inside the yard. One of the squirrel's ears had been shot. It was bloody and rather shredded.

"Poor thing," said Amber, turning the body over. The fur was still warm.

"I think it's alive!" she whispered to Wendell. "I can feel its heart beating."

They bent over the new squirrel at once, and were starting to lift it when the little animal suddenly leapt up and sat quite still on their joined hands. Perhaps it was too dazed to know where it was, though its eyes looked quick and bright. The squirrel stared at them curiously and cocked its head. Then it went down on all fours and sniffed around their palms and wrists.

"What is he doing!" Wendell whispered in delight. He couldn't help giggling because its whiskers were so tickly.

"Sh-sh!" ordered Amber, but it was too late. The squirrel jumped off their hands, bounded to the fence, and from there up a tree. As they watched, it paused and looked back at them. Then a second squirrel appeared, almost as if it had been waiting up there, and the two darted away into a green swirl of leaves.

"What a great squirrel!" Wendell crowed. "He wasn't even afraid of us. It looked like he wanted to see who we were. Is that one of the smart ones we'll be studying?"

Amber nodded.

"You know," she said, "that squirrel looked exactly like the one in the tree that came up to me and . . ." She trailed off, thoughtfully.

"Come on!" cried Wendell, pulling her along. "We've got to go see how our other squirrel is."

·UPPER·FOREST·

At a shadow past midday, after hours of tail-twitching debate, the Elders came to one of the most important decisions of their long administration. Immediately they dispatched three messenger squirrels across Forest to summon the town residents to an urgent assembly.

By that hour the day had become unbearably hot. Most mink-tails had retreated to the privacy of their nests, where they loosened leaves to let in the air, or sprawled along nearby branches. This forced the messengers to visit all corners of the wood, not just the usual seed and berry centers, and made for twice as much work.

"Everyone must be notified personally. Everyone!" the Elders had decreed. "The matter is extremely serious."

So nest to nest the steaming messengers went, sweating from their feet as, by nature, squirrels do. They told of Brown Nut's kidnapping, though most mink-tails had heard about it already. They reported the slaughter of guards and bystanders on the western edge of town that morning. (Five known dead;

several missing.) Finally, they ordered all Forest residents to go immediately—immediately!—to Great Stump, where the meeting was to be held.

"What have the Elders foreseen?" many mink-tails asked them fearfully. "Will the aliens return and drive us from our homes? How can we defend ourselves? Would it be safer to leave?"

"Go!" bellowed the messengers in irritable voices. Despite repeated foot-moppings, they were in constant danger of slipping off the branchways. "Go now to Big Stump! The answers lie there with the wise ones of our wood."

Not for many years had such a huge assembly been called. Within a short while, squirrels for miles in every direction were swarming toward Great Stump and climbing into the mighty trees surrounding the place. Their numbers went far beyond the ability of an eye to count. Woodbine and Laurel, who straggled in later than most, were astounded. They had never imagined the town to be so populous. Head upon head, haunch upon haunch, tail upon tail stretched before their dazzled eyes. Woodbine suddenly found it necessary to lean against a trunk.

"Are you all right?" Laurel asked. "That ear looks painful. I feared the worst when I saw how you were hit. You lay so still for so long on the ground."

"I'll be all right," Woodbine answered. "After this meeting, I think I'll go rest for a while in a place I know near the pond. . . . Thank you for waiting for me back there."

"Not at all. I noticed you were breathing, so I hung around. The big alien came out after his attack and threw our dead off his ground. I was afraid he would find you and finish you off."

"He is an evil alien. But the invader, well, she is a mystery." Laurel bent her ears in agreement.

"She kidnapped Brown Nut to her den, but not to kill her, I think," Woodbine went on. "Did you see how gently she carried her through the forest? And how she and her comrade picked me up just now from the ground, when they could have stamped me if they'd wanted? I had no protection."

"Who can say what goes on in this alien's mind?" Laurel replied. "While you lay in the grass, I saw other things. After the big alien had thrown our dead away, he left. Then the invader and the small alien came. They went to the field and found the bodies there. They carried them to certain bushes and laid them down out of sight—just as we would have done. Thanks to them, our dead did not lie for long in the field. Their bones are safe from scavengers and will not be disturbed."

"How amazing!" exclaimed Woodbine. "Aliens are so confusing. It is impossible to tell what they will do next." He staggered a little and gasped for air. "Whew! My head is beginning to spin. Can we find a place to sit away from these crowds?"

"Follow me," Laurel said. She led him to a perch high up in a beech tree, where he could breathe more freely. Only when he was settled did she speed off to find her own family, to assure them that she was not hurt. She was certainly a loyal friend. Woodbine closed his eyes and rested his chin on a paw.

"So!" a voice yipped behind him. "I see you have lost an ear."

"Oh, hello, Barker. I'm sure it's not as bad as that."

"But my dear fellow, I'm afraid it is. Tsk-tsk, what a mess.

This looks like the work of the treacherous invader and her band of thugs."

"Whatever it is, it's no concern of yours," Woodbine retorted. He did not like Barker staring at his wound. "I see there is not one scratch on you. And come to think of it, I didn't notice you among the troops following after Brown Nut. Weren't you one of the guards? I suppose you must have dropped off along the way before the explosions started."

"Certainly not!" Barker barked back. "I was there on the spot during the entire assault. The Elders, in fact, called me in to consult as a witness."

"Oh, is that so?"

"It is very much so."

"Then why didn't I see—"

"Are you accusing me of lying?" Barker's eyes narrowed dangerously.

"Well, I—"

"Because if you are, I would think twice about it. The Elders rely on me quite often these days, whereas I don't believe they have the least notion that you even exist."

"Why, you . . . !"

"Careful, Woodbine. You're in a weak and pitifully wounded condition."

"Why, you rat-tailed . . . !"

Barker backed away. Woodbine might be wounded, but he was not looking very pitiful. He was looking, in fact, as if he might be on the verge of a savage bite.

"Perhaps we can continue this conversation later, when you are feeling more yourself?" Barker called with a smirk as he fled out of reach.

"I am feeling exactly like myself!" bellowed Woodbine, his head beginning to spin again.

Barker was right, though. Woodbine was not acting at all like his usual self, and the trouble was not his wound. What was it about that slippery, scheming, conceited squirrel that always drove him to the brink of violence? Woodbine shivered when he thought of what he might have done—chewed up Barker's face? bitten off his tail?—if he'd lost control. Without Brown Nut to stop him, he had come closer than ever.

"I don't understand it," Woodbine murmured disgustedly to himself. "Ordinarily, I am the quietest and mildest of mink-tails. Everybody knows I wouldn't hurt a flea, even if it was crawling up my nose. But Barker is so maddening. He drives me crazy. It is really all his fault. He makes me act like a beast!"

At this moment a series of thunderous, hollow whacks rang through the air. The assembly was being officially called to order. Three more thuds (the stump was struck in unison by the powerful hind legs of several council guards) heralded the coming of the Elders. They appeared in a gleaming silver wave atop the stump and were rewarded with instant silence.

"Hear ye! Hear ye! Let it be known that . . ."

So began their speech, and the announcement of what the mink-tails of Upper Forest shortly understood to be no less than a call to battle.

Battle! Everyone looked around at one another uncomfortably. Never, in memory living or inherited, had there been such a call. Fighting was not the mink-tail habit. They were a shy lot, a teasing breed. They could harass cats out of their trees, decoy raccoons away from their nests. But battle? The silence in the trees was deafening. Couldn't they all just go home instead, and wait to see what the aliens did next?

They could not. The Elders swirled their tails militantly. Experts had been consulted. The decision was clear. It was a matter of self-protection, not to mention honor.

"What true mink-tail can sit idly by while the aliens blow friends and families from our trees?" the Elders cried, in aged, outraged voices.

"No mink-tail!" a voice called from somewhere in the crowd. "We must fight fang and claw for the safety of our wood!"

This sounded so unlike the easygoing mink-tail point of view—fang and claw? How ridiculous!—that Woodbine leaned forward to see who the voice belonged to. His gaze alighted upon . . . Barker! That scoundrel. A small group of squirrels who appeared to be his followers was cheering him loudly. Woodbine suddenly knew who the consulted "experts" were.

The Elders smiled toward Barker and waggled their long whiskers. They had not felt so powerful in years. Who could doubt now that they were in command? After that stupid mistake about the invader yesterday, some mink-tails might have questioned their fitness to lead. Thank goodness for Barker, who had told them how to fix the problem.

"What true mink-tail can shrug and turn away when a town resident has been kidnapped, when she has been dragged, kicking and screaming, to her death?" the Elders shouted forcefully together.

"No true mink-tail," cried Barker, joined by his chorus of backers. ("Not that Brown Nut was kicking or screaming,"

Woodbine muttered to himself, "or is dead . . . yet. . . ." Apparently the Elders had been given false information.)

"Fellow mink-tails!" the Elders thundered. "We believe the recent shootings and kidnappings to be part of a secret plot by aliens to eradicate us from the forest! We believe that action must be taken against this enemy. To do nothing will only invite more bloodshed!"

"Yes!" shrieked a larger mob. "We must protect ourselves!"

"Therefore, we would like to propose a plan for immediate defense against . . ."

The meeting was getting out of control, Woodbine saw. Squirrels were leaping from the trees, surrounding the stump, surging in masses across the ground. Some mink-tails were actually running over the heads of others in their eagerness to get closer to the Elders. There was no concern for the babies and the elderly in the crowd. They were being shoved aside and trampled by the rest.

Amid the shrieks and cries, the Elders continued to speak, explaining the details of their plan.

The town was to be divided into sections.

Special leaders called command minks were to be appointed to take charge of each section.

Town residents would be asked to volunteer for special section armies, to fight off alien attack if it should come again.

Section armies would be trained to kill ruthlessly to defend their home trees.

At this announcement, there was a pause in the scrambling. No one had thought of killing before. And ruthlessly? Hmm . . . But perhaps, if the home trees were really threatened . . .

"I'll volunteer!" shouted someone in the crowd.

"So will I!"

"Me too!"

There was another rush toward the stump as a horde of volunteers pushed forward. The crowd, having at first hung back, now all followed. It was as if a single mind had been persuaded, and now a single, ten-thousand-footed animal surrounded Great Stump awaiting further orders.

"May Spring Follow Winter as Day Follows Dark," the Elders intoned at this juncture, preparing to leave the scene. The chant only drove the crowds wilder.

Woodbine began to creep away. Armies? Command minks? He looked about in amazement. His ear was throbbing, and perhaps he was not seeing clearly. The assembly seemed to have turned into a riot. Brown Nut was forgotten. Her name was a rallying cry, but not a single plan for her rescue had been put forth. Below, in the clearing, battle troops were beginning to form. The command minks had been named and were in conference with the Elders. Barker was one, of course.

"Wait!" Woodbine couldn't help calling out. "What about Brown Nut? And I am not sure the aliens are plotting what you think. Today I had a most unusual meeting with . . ." His voice was drowned out.

"Also, they have weapons! Terrible weapons!" he shouted a bit later.

"Oh, hush yourself," said a mink-tail who was descending slowly through the beech toward the ground. Woodbine saw it was the old firebrand he'd talked to in the white oak just after Brown Nut had been carried off.

"You're too young to know what you're saying," the fellow

went on. "This sort of thing has happened hundreds of times in other places. I've traveled around, and I know. Everybody gets invaders from time to time. Everyone gets kidnappers. They always make a point of doing something about them. All these tall trees have kept Forest in the dark ages when it comes to battle. Nobody's had to lift a paw. But the world is changing. We can't afford to sit back anymore. Starting an army is the best idea the Elders have had in years. Come on down with me and join up. It'll be a great adventure, you'll see."

With a look of disbelief, Woodbine turned and fled toward the pond.

·LOWER·FOREST·

"Hello? I'd like to speak to Chief Teckstar, please. Is he there?"

Mr. Padgett leaned back in his swivel chair, fingering the telephone cord. He was at his desk, at work. Around him, workers at other desks crouched over piles of paper or in front of computer keyboards. The air-conditioning system moaned in the background. Outside, the sun had turned furiously hot.

"Hello, Teckstar? Len Padgett here. I just wanted to call and say how much Mrs. Padgett and I appreciate the fine effort you made yesterday trying to find our little runaway. . . . Yes, I guess they told you. She spent the night in the woods. . . . No, no, she's fine. Not a scratch on her. Of course, her mother and I are kind of shot up after . . . What? Oh no, she was never in any kind of danger. No danger at all. I found her early this morning, stuck up a tree, and brought her home safe and sound. She was mighty glad to see me. But there's something else I wanted to talk to you about. . . ."

Mr. Padgett swiveled his chair around so that his back was to a glassed-in compartment on one side of the room. It was the office of the department boss, Mr. Wick. Mr. Padgett was not supposed to use his desk telephone for personal calls.

"I wonder if," Mr. Padgett began, "I wonder if, by any chance, you've noticed a rather frightening surge in Forest's squirrel population lately? Yes . . . well . . . perhaps *frightening* is the wrong word. Nevertheless, there seem to be many more of the mangy little pests than usual. I was thinking we men might get together to see if we can't bring the number down a bit, for the safety of our town and our children and our . . .

"What? . . . Well, a shooting party was what I had in mind. We could put aside a weekend and make a point of going after them. I've got a shotgun, and a good many other men in town have them, too. . . . Oh, I see. . . ."

Mr. Padgett swiveled around in his chair to check on Mr. Wick. The old geezer seemed to have wandered out of his office. There was no sign of him anywhere.

"Look, Teckstar. I'm not suggesting a 'massacre,' as you put it," Mr. Padgett went on, his voice rising. "Just a little sensible shooting with the idea of cutting the head count down to where the poor things won't have to starve to death this winter. There's too many of them, that's the trouble. Why, I was out in my yard this morning and saw several huge packs sitting up in the tress. And that's nothing compared to what's back there in the woods. There's thousands back there, and they're strong breeders, let me say. Nothing stops a red-blooded squirrel from . . . What's that?"

Mr. Padgett began to swivel his chair rapidly back and forth. He had never liked Chief Teckstar. The man couldn't take an honest suggestion. He didn't like to listen to reason.

"I know that Mother Nature takes care of things like squirrel populations!" Mr. Padgett bellowed into the receiver. "Do you think I've got the brain of a beetle? I just thought we might like to help her out a little, before the situation gets any worse!"

Mr. Padgett gave one final, powerful swivel that spun his chair all the way around. Then he glanced up. Good grief! Every face in the room was turned toward his desk. Everyone was staring straight at him. It was just like the scene in his yard that morning, when all those pesky squirrels had surrounded him and stared at him as if he'd done something terrible. And then he had! He'd gone out and almost shot his own daughter! Those horrid pests had gone and made him shoot his own . . .

"Mr. Padgett, may I please have a word with you in my office?" said a quiet voice behind him.

Mr. Padgett jumped and whirled around. "Uh, Mr. Wick!" The old turnip was quick as a cat. He'd crept up behind him without the smallest noise. Mr. Padgett's face turned bright red. Forgetting to say good-bye to Chief Teckstar, he hung up the phone.

"This way, Mr. Padgett, if you would be so kind," said Mr. Wick in his quietest and most deadly voice.

Mr. Padgett stood up with pounding heart. He hadn't felt so frightened since the sixth grade, when Mrs. Ramsbottom had caught him and sent him to the principal's office for drawing those awful pictures of her during math class.

◆ ◆ ◆

"So, Dad, did you have to take the pictures with you to the principal's office?" Amber asked at dinner that night, after

Mr. Padgett had told them all about Mr. Wick and Mrs. Ramsbottom and his dreadful day at work. Luckily, he had not been fired, only shamed and dishonored and publicly cut down to beetle size.

"Huh? What?" Mr. Padgett looked exhausted. There were circles under his eyes.

"You know, the bad pictures you drew," said Wendell, sitting forward eagerly. "Did you have to show them to the principal?"

"Well, I—"

"Now, children," Mrs. Padgett broke in. "That is not something you need to know. That is something from the deep, dark past. Your father is upset and—"

"Well, at least tell us what the bad pictures looked like!" Wendell couldn't help exclaiming. "Was Mrs. Ramsbottom topless, or bottomless, or wearing purple underwear, or—"

"Wendell! Please hush!" said his mother, but Wendell went right on.

"Listen, yesterday I saw this picture in a magazine at the drugstore? It was of a lady in a sports car advertisement who was completely naked except for the teeniest, weeniest, little pair of pink—"

"Wendell! That is quite enough!"

"They weren't what you think," Wendell said indignantly. "They were only—"

"*Wendell!*" Mrs. Padgett's fork clattered to her plate.

Mr. Padgett stood up abruptly and left the table.

Amber pushed her chair back and got up, too.

"Come on, Wendell, we've got work to do," she said. "But

first let's help Mom with the dishes. Looks like everybody's had a hard day today."

Mrs. Padgett smiled gratefully at her daughter.

"The dishes! Forget it!" cried Wendell. "I never do the dishes. I'm only a little kid."

"Listen!" Amber whispered when she had pulled him out to the kitchen. "There've been hundreds of squirrels rustling around in our trees all afternoon. I want to take the little squirrel back to her own people tonight, before anyone gets upset. If you want to come, too, and spend the night outside with me . . ."

"Mom will never let me. She thinks I'm a baby."

"I repeat: if you want to spend the night outside with me, you must help me do the dishes. Right now. And look happy about it, okay?" Amber said fiercely.

"This is stupid," Wendell whispered back, but he took up a dish towel.

Not more than ten minutes later, Amber had negotiated the deal. "He's old enough—look at him," she said, while Wendell tried to smile and dry a pot at the same time. "And besides, I'll be there to look after him."

"Well, all right," murmured their mother feebly. Wendell nearly dropped the pot. "And thank you again, dear ones, for taking care of the dishes." She put an arm around Wendell. "It was so very, very, very, very thoughtful of you both."

She might have gone on for several more delirious sentences if another loud rustling noise hadn't suddenly risen outside the house. They all stopped to listen. It sounded like the passing of hundreds of feet overhead, or the thrashing of disturbed branches, or the chatter of little voices. Perhaps it was all three at once.

"There go those squirrels again," Mrs. Padgett said, looking up. "I swear there seem to be more of them all the time!"

◆

The sun had no sooner set over Goodspeed Hill than two plans went into operation at the Padgett house. Amber was in charge of both, to Wendell's great delight.

"The first is the cover plan, the one we say we're doing and pretend to carry out," Amber explained in a low voice in the upstairs bathroom, where they had gone to talk. "It is that we're sleeping out in the field tonight and will be back for breakfast in the morning. The second plan is the real one, the one the first plan turns into after everyone is asleep."

"Oh, wow!" Wendell couldn't help screaming.

"*Sh-sh-sh!*"

No one knew how to run an operation better than Amber. She was a master of detail, a maestro of design, a thinker of dazzling cleverness. This, anyway, was how Wendell saw his sister, especially now that she had managed to liberate him from the house and the bedtime clutches of his mother.

"Where are we going to sleep? In a tree?" he demanded.

"Sh-sh! Your voice is much louder than you think. People can hear you for miles. If you want to pull off a plan, the first trick you have to learn is how to whisper," Amber whispered. "You know how Mom always seems to know what you're going to do before you do it? Guess how she finds out."

"She hears me say it?"

"That's right. She has ears."

"Weird! Well, how's this?" Wendell said in a sort of scratchy growl. He hadn't practiced whispering very much. Yelling had solved most of his problems in the past.

"Better. Now listen."

Amber explained the plans that would shortly unfold, including a part Wendell particularly loved in which they stuffed their sleeping bags with clothes to make it look as if they were still in them. Twenty minutes later they marched out the back door, carrying knapsacks, sleeping bags, and a mass of blankets toward the field.

"Have a good time," Mrs. Padgett's cheerful voice rang out behind them. "And, Amber, please remember to get that other sleeping bag down from the tree tomorrow. It'll be ruined if it stays up there much longer."

"Sorry, Mom. I forgot all about it. I'll get it tomorrow, I promise."

"I bet you didn't really forget about it, did you?" Wendell growled in his new gravelly voice as they tramped away.

"No, I didn't," Amber said.

"You left it up there on purpose so we could go back, right?"

"Right."

Wendell shivered with pleasure. "Did you bring the little squirrel?"

"She's in a shoe box in my knapsack."

"Won't Mom notice she's gone?"

"I don't think so. She's got to take care of Dad. He's in bad shape. She'll have to use all her energy putting him back together by morning. That's why she probably won't bother checking on us, either, so our plans will work."

"But even if she does check on us, she'll think we're still there because of . . . "

"The stuffed sleeping bags, right. Look out. Your voice is starting to screech again."

"Oh. Sorry." Wendell pounded himself on the head and hunched down toward his sneakers. It seemed to help lower his tone.

"Amber?" he rasped. "How do you know stuff like this? I can never figure it out."

She shrugged. "I guess I just watch. You know, if you're jumping around and yelling all the time, you can't see anything, but everyone can see you. But if you're quiet, and stay off to one side, then you can see things and hear things, and people won't know you know."

This was information that would have been lost on Wendell an hour ago. Now, in the thick silence of the night field, a small moon of understanding began to rise in his mind. When Amber shortly said, "Okay, it's time to head into the forest. Keep your eyes open and your mouth shut," he knew exactly what she meant.

"Maybe we'll hear the squirrels speak their own language," he croaked. "Maybe we'll be able to figure out what they're saying."

"Maybe," whispered Amber. "Now sh-sh-sh!"

They tramped through the woods for what seemed a long time. Dim moonlight filtered through the branches. They navigated with the help of a small flashlight that Amber had brought. The forest sounds were eerie. Hoots and strange howls, flutters and coughs, squeals and mysterious thumps erupted from the dark all around them. Wendell had a sudden vision of an undiscovered, alien world working away just beyond their rim of sight.

"Amber?"

"Sh-sh!"

Without warning, something dropped in their path. Amber leapt back, pulling Wendell with her. But when they recovered their breaths, they saw it was only a rotten branch. Nothing to worry about. Wendell's hands were sweaty. He wiped them on his jeans and set off after his sister again. He had left his knapsack back with the sleeping bags in the field. (It had made an amazingly real-looking human head for the bag.) But Amber was wearing her knapsack. She was walking carefully, he saw, because the little squirrel was inside. Her sneakers made almost no noise as they passed under the trees. Wendell's feet, on the other hand, kept getting tangled in bushes, which he then had to wrench free of, which caused a lot of thrashing and delay as they went along.

"How do you . . . ?"

"Take smaller steps," Amber whispered. She touched his head protectively. "Don't worry, you're doing great."

They reached the tree with the rope. Amber handed it to Wendell.

"You go up first," she whispered.

"How?"

"Shinny! Like you do at the firehouse."

Wendell had spent a fair amount of time practicing shinnying up the firehouse pole over the years. He had no trouble pulling himself up the rope, which was thinner but far less slick. But when he arrived on the first branch, he took a wrong step, fell over, and just barely saved himself from plunging to the ground by grabbing a smaller limb with one hand.

"Good grief! Are you all right?" Amber hissed from below.

"Yes."

"Hold on tight. Here I come."

The sleeping bag was still nailed up, exactly as Amber had left it.

"Look. Squirrel droppings. They've been using this place," she exclaimed.

"Oh no."

"It's good. It means they're interested in us. They've been checking us out. Also, they'll find the little squirrel faster if we have to leave her here. She's still sort of wobbly and probably can't walk too well."

Amber opened the knapsack while Wendell brushed off the sleeping bag and crawled out on it.

"This is the greatest. The greatest!" he cheered. "I'm in a secret tree house! No, I'm on a flying carpet heading for the moon! No, I'm a squirrel who lives up here and runs in the trees and I've never, never touched the ground in my whole—"

"Wendell! You are waking up every animal in this forest."

"Oops . . . sorry."

Amber took the shoe box out of her knapsack, then removed a rubber band and the cover, which was punctured with holes. The little squirrel was crouched inside, her eyes wide and worried.

"Okay, you can go," Amber said. "Go on. Go back to your friends."

The squirrel's tail quivered a little. Otherwise she didn't move.

"I was afraid of this," Amber said. "She's still sort of in

shock, I guess. She probably thinks we'll shoot her if she starts to run away."

"Well, just let her stay there, then," Wendell said. "She'll get up her courage after a while."

So Amber crawled out on the sleeping bag with Wendell, and they both lay back and put their hands behind their heads.

"Don't worry. The sleeping bag will hold," Amber whispered. "It's made of Gore-Tex. Also, I used a ton of nails and really hammered them in well."

"Mom will love you."

"I guess we have to wait now, and see what happens," Amber said. She gazed through the branches toward the starry sky overhead. The moon looked brighter and bigger, as if they were a lot closer to it than they'd been on the ground.

"Isn't it nice up here?" she asked. "So quiet and friendly feeling. Maybe it's the last truly peaceful place in the world, and these squirrels are the only ones who know about it. They could probably tell us a few things if we'd let them."

"Sh-sh! I've been hearing rustling sounds," Wendell whispered.

"Where?"

"Everywhere. All around."

They lay side by side in silence. The leaves were like a curtain surrounding them. Occasionally they fluttered or twitched, as if something was passing in back of them.

"I have the weirdest feeling we're being watched," Wendell rasped.

"Look!" Amber pointed up.

Small, dark shapes appeared suddenly in the branches over

their heads. The shapes swirled and leapt about, and dropped closer to them.

"This is quite unusual," Amber's voice said in Wendell's ear. "I didn't expect any action. Squirrels don't like the dark. They can't see in it. Like us, only worse. They don't ordinarily go out at night."

"Well," said Wendell in his regular voice, "there sure are a whole lot of them out here now. There are more over there, and some more coming up on us from below. And there's a big black mass of something creeping across from those trees on the right. . . ."

Amber sprang up.

"Wendell, I think we should get out of here," she said in a low voice. "Something strange is happening." An odd chittery sound had begun and was swelling louder and coming near. "The squirrels are upset. Come on. Let's start climbing down. Move slowly, okay?"

"Okay."

Wendell inched himself off the sleeping bag. Amber put on her knapsack and was about to follow when she remembered the little squirrel. She reached for the shoe box, and was placing it gently in the middle of the sleeping bag, where it would be safe, when—the attack struck. Squirrels flew at them from all directions, landing on their shoulders and backs, the tops of their heads.

"Help!" Wendell screamed. "They're all over me!"

They were all over Amber, too. She tried to bat them away, but there were too many. Their nails were sharp and scratched through her shirt. Amber dropped the shoe box and watched in horror as it toppled and fell off the edge of the sleeping bag.

"Ow! Ow!" Below her in the tree, Wendell was squirming and twisting.

"Jump!" Amber yelled to him. "Don't use the rope. Jump!"

"I can't!" he screeched. "They're getting in my face. I can't see."

Amber struggled down toward him, carrying what seemed to be five or six squirrels with her. She covered her brother's head with her arms and beat at the mass of darting creatures. Their fur felt slippery. A frightening smell of wild animal rose up her nose.

The squirrels began to fall away. One last one clung to Wendell's collar. She grasped it by the back and yanked it off.

"Now, Wendell! Jump!" she cried, and more or less flung him from the tree. Then she hurled herself off the branch. A thick layer of cool air gushed past her as she fell through the dark toward the ground.

·UPPER·FOREST·

News of the defeat of two dangerous aliens who had crept into town after dark and hidden out in the invader's abandoned nest flew across Upper Forest with the first rays of morning light. Many mink-tails were excited by the victory, which showed how well the town could defend itself against outsiders when the need arose.

But many others were frightened. The return of the aliens, one of whom was rumored to be the deadly invader herself, was widely viewed as a declaration of war. Why else would the aliens have come back except to spy and plot more mink-tail murders?

"They are after our hides, no doubt about it," Barker told an official group of command minks who had gathered in the white oak to examine the battle site. "The Elders are in total agreement on this point."

By some means not entirely clear, Barker had managed to put himself in charge of the other command minks and their operations. He was now Supreme Commander Barker, who spoke hourly to the Elders. They relied on his advice.

"And the sure sign of the aliens' intentions is this," he went on. "That they brought their prisoner with them to dangle cruelly under the noses of our troops."

"You mean Brown Nut? She is still alive, then?" a command mink in charge of the pond quadrant inquired.

"She was alive when last seen," Barker corrected. "The aliens brought her confined in a box, which they flung to the ground when our attack began. Later they were seen dragging poor Brown Nut away again. She remains in their hands, suffering who knows what tortures."

"Ach! It is bad. What is the world coming to when such barbarians rise up to occupy our trees?"

"What it is coming to," said Barker, with a cool flick of his tail, "is that stronger action must be taken. It is no longer enough to think simply of defending ourselves. We mink-tails must sharpen our wits and go actively on the attack if we are to survive."

Several command minks groaned when they heard this. Their troops had so little experience with military action. It was hard enough to organize the daily marches around Forest's perimeters and to keep the volunteer lookouts awake at night. To have to go further, into the planning and carrying out of ambushes and attacks, well, when would anyone have time to sleep?

"I should think after last night the aliens would see the madness of continuing their invasions," the command mink in charge of the Random River quadrant piped up. "Perhaps they will just stop. And then we can stop. And then life can go on as it did before: peacefully and independently on both sides."

Barker sized up the speaker with quick eyes and made a mental note to replace this commander. He would advise the Elders about it that very day. No weak or spiritless leadership could be tolerated in the mink-tail army. The future of Forest's mink-tails depended on it, not to mention the future of the Supreme Commander (ahem). After all his hard work persuading the Elders to trust him and do what he said, Barker wasn't about to let this war fizzle out.

He narrowed his eyes and addressed the Random River command mink sternly.

"Be careful, Officer! Your words sound remarkably like those of the traitor and coward Woodbine. His own sister is kidnapped, and yet he refuses to join our troops. Do you know that he goes out to the pond every day to sleep in a blackberry bush? His family is disgraced. His sister is abandoned. Meanwhile, he complains that he does not believe in fighting. Hah! He is afraid, as everyone knows. One little ear blown off and he runs away to hide."

"It is said that Woodbine speaks admiringly of the invader," the pond-quadrant command mink said. "Can this be true?"

"I can say no more than that we are watching him," Barker replied. "If he should try to contact the aliens again, for any reason, we would be forced to take quick and drastic action."

"Contact them again! Does that mean he has been passing information to the Lower Region?"

"Draw your own conclusions. I must be silent for reasons of mink-tail security," Barker replied in such disturbing tones that the command minks looked at one another in alarm.

"And now let us turn our minds to nobler things—to the waging of war!" the Supreme Commander commanded. "The Lower Region may have its blasting weapons, but we have our numbers. Our army is truly massive. It is training now to travel in power swarms through our trees and to strike like lightning. The aliens are few, by comparison, and separated by their box nests.

"Despite our brilliant victory against the invader and her sidekick last night, our future strategy will not be to attack the aliens directly," Barker went on. "They are larger and stronger. Our goal will be to destroy their living systems. For instance, there is a juice that runs through the wires along their paths and roadways. Their nests are addicted to it. They quickly shut down when the juice is interrupted."

A juice? The command minks were amazed to hear of such a thing. They had traveled these wires for years, and never guessed. They knew so little about the Lower Region. They had not really thought of it as a place before. Barker had certainly done his homework.

He continued briskly, "I have discovered also that the aliens' communication systems are extremely primitive. They depend on complex sending and receiving devices that most aliens cannot understand. One small malfunction and crunch!—the device is out of order. Then no one can fix it until specialists are called in. And what if the paths and roadways have been blocked by various means I have in mind?

"Command minks, draw near! The time has come for us to begin work on a plan that, if successful, will drive these barbarian aliens from the town of Forest—forever!"

The command minks were so impressed by this forceful

speech that they came forward to applaud the Supreme Commander.

"Hooray, Barker!"

"This is clear thinking, I must say."

"Congratulations, old chap!"

"You know, I believe we may have a chance of defeating these evil aliens!"

"A chance! It's a sure thing!"

• ◆ •

From the center of a blackberry bush somewhere in the Second Quadrant:

"Well, Laurel, this town is certainly heading for trouble."

"Oh, Woodbine! I'm so scared!"

"The mink-tails of Forest are going to war for the first time in our long and quiet history."

"It's unbelievable. Our troops are massing even now."

"Who knows what will happen next. We may be defeated and driven from our trees. Our town may be destroyed by alien weapons. Even if we win—for Barker is a brilliant commander, a military genius, it is said—even then, many hundreds of mink-tails will be killed in battle. Those who survive will live on, alone, weeping for their lost ones."

"My whole family has volunteered for the army! My mother, my father, my sisters and brothers. They say all those things will happen if we don't fight. The aliens have plans to wipe us out. We must attack first if we are to win and save ourselves."

"Rubbish and corn rot! Barker and his power-hungry friends have invented these tales to frighten us."

"I'm not so sure. The aliens might not be as innocent as

you think, Woodbine. Anyway, why would Barker and his friends wish to frighten us?"

"They want to go to war, for their own purposes. They like giving orders and being in charge, and are probably plotting to get rid of the Elders as soon as they can."

"I don't know. It's so hard to see clearly."

"If only we could speak to the invader. Though she is young, she is powerful. I've seen her eyes. She would not be in favor of this war and might help us try to avoid it."

"Speak to the invader! Woodbine, are you crazy? How could we talk to such a strange being? Have you forgotten how she kidnapped your sister and still holds her captive?"

"I believe the invader was bringing Brown Nut back to us when Barker's troops struck last night."

"How do you know? The aliens act in confusing ways—you said it yourself."

"I was there watching. I saw how the invader came with her companion, the little alien. While our army was scrambling into formation, I saw how carefully she climbed the tree, carrying a pouch on her back. When she reached her nest, I saw her take a box from the pouch and open it with gentlest fingers. Inside was Brown Nut. I saw the invader speak to my sister and tell her to go free."

"But, Woodbine, how do you know what she said? No one understands the aliens' bubbling noises. Maybe the invader was planning to make Brown Nut into an example by slaughtering her before our eyes."

"There are some things that can be understood no matter what the language."

"For a dreamer, Woodbine, you are certainly wide-awake."

"Laurel, you are my only friend. I have a plan. Will you come with me to visit the invader?"

"But that is more dangerous than battle. The invader was wounded last night. Reports say she lies in her nest, surrounded by killer aliens. Also, Barker is watching you. One false move and he will have you arrested."

"Will you come, anyway? We'll try to sneak past the guard-minks. It's our only chance to rescue Brown Nut before the war begins."

"War! What have we idiot mink-tails come to?"

"Please, please say yes? I would feel so much better if you came along."

"Of course I'll come. But I think we may be sorry we ever left this blackberry bush."

·LOWER·FOREST·

Amber Padgett leaned back against pillows and stared up at the ceiling of her room. It was the only place she could look comfortably, aching as she did in every bone and joint. She'd spent all of yesterday lying in bed and still felt no better this morning. The fall from the white oak tree had been a hard one.

Across the room, the little squirrel was curled up asleep in the hamster cage. She had eaten a good breakfast of dried corn and raisins. Now she seemed in no worse condition than before her tumble from the tree two nights ago. Perhaps, Amber thought, the box had softened her landing. Wendell had found her cowering inside it on the ground and insisted on bringing her home again.

Nothing had cushioned Amber's fall. A bandage across her chin covered a gash that had needed ten stitches to close. Her left wrist was fractured and encased to the elbow in a cast. Two back teeth were cracked from her chin's impact with the ground. (The dentist would see to them later, when she could open her mouth.) Finally, her head throbbed from a concussion that the doctor had called "worth watching."

"You were lucky not to break your neck," he said. "And what are these odd little bites all over your shoulders?"

She had refused to answer. Wendell had done it for her, the double-crossing rat. Except for a scratch across one cheek, he was hardly hurt at all. Not even a sprained ankle.

"Wendell is younger. And softer," Amber's mother explained. "I suppose he just sort of bounced."

Mrs. Padgett was being a most attentive nurse, always hovering in the bedroom door, trying to be cheerful. She appeared now, wiping her hands on a dish towel.

"Amber dear, can I bring you some more chicken noodle soup?"

"No, thank you."

"Another magazine or a book?"

"No."

"A puzzle, a sweater, a radio, a—"

"Mother! I'm all right!"

"Well, you can't mope around all day again staring at the ceiling."

"Why not? It's the only thing I *can* do." Tears welled up in Amber's eyes. She turned her head away to hide them.

A small breeze came through the half-open window, flapping the torn screen to and fro. Outside, Amber saw a flash of green go by, disappear, then flash by again. It looked like a tree branch signaling in the wind.

"Tell Wendell to come," she told her mother suddenly.

"Wendell! I thought you were never going to talk to him again. I thought he was on your permanent blacklist."

"He is. Tell him to come, anyway. Soon."

He arrived half an hour later—slouched in, his eyes on the floor. Amber saw that he was on the verge of tears himself, this soft brother, this bendable, traitorous one.

"So what's happening out in the world?" she asked him coldly.

"Oh, Amber, I'm so sorry. Please, please don't be mad. I didn't mean to tell about the squirrels. Mom and Dad got it out of me. I was upset, and they made me tell."

"Who says I'm mad?" Amber inquired. "Did I say I was mad?"

"No." Wendell sniffed. "But you are."

"I'm not mad at all, actually," Amber said with a painful clench of her jaw. "I'm just . . ." She looked over at the little squirrel sleeping safely in her cage.

"Furious! I know!" wailed Wendell. "I was so stupid!" He pounded himself on the head. "I should have said we just fell out of the tree. I shouldn't have told about the squirrels attacking us. Now Dad is going to—"

"Sh-sh-sh!" Amber put her good hand over his mouth. "What's done is done. Right now I need information. What's going on? Mom won't tell me a thing. Is Dad on the warpath?"

"Yes!"

"I thought so."

"He's over talking to Chief Teckstar."

"I knew it."

"I heard him on the phone yesterday. He's going to organize a search-and-destroy mission."

"A what!"

"You know, like in the movies. Search-and-destroy. I heard

him talking about the squirrels, how there are too many of them, and they have gotten sick, and now they are attacking people and need to be stopped. He wants to clean out the forest, that's what he said. He told Chief Teckstar it was time to clean their clocks."

"Clean their clocks! Good grief!"

"I don't get it," Wendell said after a brief pause. "Do the squirrels have clocks?"

Amber knotted her fist and struck it on the mattress.

"It's an expression," she explained. "It means that Dad has flipped out. He's taking this squirrel attack personally."

"I still don't get it."

"Listen, Wendell. These squirrels don't have clocks. What they do have is minds. They're smart. They attacked us because they were frightened and wanted to protect themselves. We were invading their trees, right? Anyone would be terrified after Dad's shoot-out in the backyard."

"But I thought you said the squirrels would understand," Wendell said. "You know, because we buried their dead ones."

"Well, they didn't see us do it. Or they didn't like how we did it," Amber said. "Or something. Whatever it is, they're frightened and angry. But that is no reason to kill them off. We've got to stop this search-and-destroy mission."

"But how?"

"Sh-sh. Let me think."

In the silence following this command, Wendell began to hear soft noises coming from the window. At first he thought it was the wind rustling through the broken screen. But when he turned to look, he saw that the edge of the screen had flapped wide open. Just inside, cautiously sniffing and crouching, were two small gray squirrels, their tails rising behind them like fine sprays of mist.

Wendell was so amazed that he could not speak. He simply froze, sitting on the end of Amber's bed. But perhaps some invisible current of excitement made its way to his sister, because a moment later she looked up and spied the intruders, too.

Did the squirrels know they were being watched? They investigated the windowsill with nervous sniffs, then jumped down on top of a bookcase that ran underneath. A lopsided stack of paperbacks caught the interest of one. It nibbled the edge of a page. The other examined an electric pencil sharpener of Amber's that hadn't worked for several months. Its quick squirrel eye followed the cord down to where it was still plugged into the outlet, uselessly, after all this time. Then the little creature sat up on its haunches and looked straight at Wendell.

Zap! Wendell was almost knocked over by the intelligence of its gaze. The squirrel had not stumbled through the window by chance.

Amber cleared her throat. "It's my squirrel!" she whispered to Wendell. "See his ear? He's the same one we picked up in the yard, the same one that came to study me, close up, in the tree. I'm sure of it now."

Amazing but true. The squirrel staring at Wendell had only one ear. There was a ragged place where the other ear had been. The wound still showed. The other squirrel, his companion, jumped gracefully to his side and sat up, too. It was more elegantly made, with finer ears and dark-furred feet. Now that Amber had recognized the first squirrel, the particular markings on the second were easy to see.

"Why are they here?" Wendell rasped.

Amber nodded at the hamster cage. The little squirrel was no longer asleep. She was up, peering at the newcomers, her sinewy squirrel paws gripping the bars. Standing that way, on her haunches, she looked so much like a small person—a small, furry person with bright eyes and a cap—that Amber felt a twinge for having ever shut her in. The more she saw of these squirrels, the more like people they seemed.

The two on the bookcase had begun another round of sniffing and probing. They were thorough and businesslike and showed extraordinary balance in their small, quick steps. Nothing on the cluttered bookcase top was knocked over, or as much as jostled. Their long, full-bodied tails were feather-light. Like banners, they floated above the two busy heads, registering surprise, curiosity, uncertainty, distrust.

Amber and Wendell were so afraid of frightening the little animals that they hardly dared to breathe during these investigations. Finally they were rewarded. Both squirrels sprang off the bookcase and ran in one sweep past the bed to the hamster cage. Amber's squirrel jumped on top of it, while the other went so close to the little squirrel that they seemed to brush noses. Then there was a great flicking of tails.

"I think they know each other!" Wendell whispered in delight.

But the best part was still to come. With their greetings finished, the three squirrels gathered close together, or as close as was possible with one barred away from the others. A strange series of noises, half chirp, half mew, rose out of their huddle, and it became clear that a conference of some sort was under way. What was being discussed the children couldn't tell. Nor were they prepared for the next moment, when all three squirrels turned as one and fixed them with powerful, dark eyes.

A low, chittery whir began. Amber and Wendell, who had heard this very sound in the tree, moments before the squirrels' nighttime attack, shrank back. But soon the sound climbed to a higher key. It wavered and warbled on a thin edge, swelled, and fanned out like a fountain of water. It shrilled, then quieted . . . softened . . . became mysterious. . . . With light steps, it dropped down to lower platforms of tone.

Wendell sat enthralled. He had never heard anything like it in his life. Amber, recalling how the old silver-haired squirrels had chittered in a single voice when they came to look at her that first morning in the tree, leaned forward and tried to trace meanings in the sounds. This was language, she understood. She and Wendell were being spoken to. They were being informed of certain facts or shown certain views or warned of certain dangers or . . . what? Amber strained to understand. She knew it was important, but there was nothing she could catch hold of to make the translation begin.

The squirrels' performance continued. Their voices synchronized perfectly. No single one stood out from the others. All blended into a wondrous flow of sound, a surge that Wendell would later describe as "music" and that Amber turned around and around in her mind. Where did the secret of their speech lie? If not in words, then in what? In rhythm or pitch? In loudness or vibration? She wondered if her ears simply could not hear this language. Perhaps its patterns and meanings were beyond the human range.

The voices sank lower, to the deep-chested whir of the beginning. Then all stopped at once and the squirrels posed silently for a few moments, before coming down on all fours again. On the bed, Amber moved her legs under the blankets, and Wendell touched his hands to his ears.

The visitor squirrels swirled around the hamster cage for another minute or so, then leapt off the low table and made for the bookcase and the windowsill. Amber took this opportunity to ease out of bed. She padded across the rug to the cage and opened the sliding door in its front.

"Go on, little squirrel. Go off with your friends. They came especially to get you, I think."

The squirrel drew away shyly when she spoke. But when Amber continued to stand motionless, holding the door up, she crept forward and sniffed the opening. She put her front feet over the entrance, brought her back feet out with a hop, and halted suspiciously. Encouraging chirps erupted from the two watching by the window. The little squirrel jumped to the floor and joined them in a flash on the sill. A second later, all three had disappeared through the screen, and a patter of paws rose overhead from the roof.

Amber let the door slide back in place and turned to Wendell.

"I have a plan," she announced. "Are you ready to go to work?"

"Ready," breathed Wendell. "Tell me anything. I'll do it."

"You'll have to do a little spying for me this afternoon. And we're getting up early tomorrow morning. Really early, before sunrise."

"Before sunrise! Oh, wow! Are we going to run away?"

"Sh-sh-sh!"

Wendell clapped his hand over his mouth.

"We are not going to run away. We are taking a trip on the bus to Randomville," Amber whispered.

"Weird!" Wendell gazed at his sister. "But why?"

"You know that man who wrote my library book?"

"What book?"

"*Woodland Animals and Their Habitats*. Remember? Professor A. B. Spark, who teaches at the university. I was thinking that he might like to study our squirrels."

"But *we're* studying our squirrels," Wendell objected. "And we haven't even started yet. We don't want a lot of other people coming around and—"

"Wendell, listen. There are times when the best thing to do is go for help. We're in one of those times. If we don't get some help on our side, fast, there won't be any squirrels to study. My idea is to somehow convince Professor Spark of how smart our squirrels are. Then maybe he'll want to study them. And if he wants to study them, then he might help us stop the search-and-destroy mission."

Wendell shook his head. "How do you even know he still lives in Randomville? This book looks old."

Amber shrugged. "We'll see."

"And if he is still there, how will we find out where he lives? And then how will we get to it? Anyway, he's probably too important to speak to us. Or maybe he hates squirrels. Or children. Or he was knocked unconscious in a car crash and can't hear or see or think or . . ."

Amber laughed at this feeble list of doubts. What did Wendell think she was, some kind of small-time operator? No! She was a master of detail, a maestro of design, a thinker of dazzling cleverness, etc., and so on. Hadn't she already proved it a hundred times?

Wendell sighed and nodded.

Well, then . . .

Amber ordered the phone book brought to her and demanded a report on Mrs. Padgett's whereabouts. (In the kitchen.) She sent Wendell to the fire station to spy on the search-and-destroy mission and report back. She found a map of Randomville on her father's bedside table, called the bus station for departure times, stowed travel clothing under her bed, took out her wallet and counted her money ($14.26), and pretended to be asleep when her mother came in to check on her. (In fact, she was feeling remarkably wide-awake. And better.)

Seconds later, she was at her desk writing furiously in a notebook. Luckily, her left wrist was the broken one, and she was right-handed.

Or was it luck? Wendell's eyes followed his sister. He closed his mouth, sharpened his wits, and did as he was told. He had a lot to learn, he could see that now. Amber was miles ahead of him in figuring out the world. She understood grown-ups and knew how to get things done. She'd stopped being mad, too. Or had she? Wendell couldn't tell anymore. She was keeping her thoughts inside, where he couldn't see.

"Wendell! What's happening down at the fire station?"

"They're going tomorrow morning to clean out the forest. Chief Teckstar agreed. They're taking their guns."

"Tomorrow morning! That doesn't give us very much time."

"Couldn't we just go to Dad and everybody and tell them to stop?" Wendell asked. He was beginning to feel nervous about the bus trip to Randomville. "We could explain how the squirrels have been there for ages, and how smart they are, and how they just got scared."

"It wouldn't work," Amber said. "We aren't old enough to make it work. Nobody in this town takes us seriously. That's the price you pay when you're a kid. It doesn't mean we have to give up, though. Guess what? I found Professor Spark's address in the phone book."

"But how can we just go barging in on him?" Wendell complained. "He doesn't even know us!"

"All the better," Amber said with a wise nod. Then she lay back suddenly against the pillows. "Oof! My head is starting to hurt again. I guess I overdid it. Listen, I've got to take a rest. Will you keep an eye on things for the next couple of hours?"

Wendell was so pleased with this request, which seemed to show that Amber's trust in him had returned, that he reported to the backyard immediately for duty. Unfortunately, nothing was happening. The sun was hot. The bushes were limp. He lay down on his back in the shade and looked up at the sky.

There was a rustling noise coming from the forest. Wendell cocked his head. It sounded like a wave. Or rather, like a series of waves, dashing against the rocks on a craggy shore. He sat up. The rustling grew louder. He stood and gazed across the field. A thick stream of shapes was flowing through the trees over there. Squirrels!

Wendell climbed the fence and began to cross the field. He kept well back and hid behind bushes when he could. Not that he was afraid. He wanted to observe the squirrels without being seen by them. Where were they going in such numbers? The stream went on and on. What were they planning? He knew they could be fierce and violent. Now they seemed calm, orderly, engrossed in their own mysterious reasons.

Amber said she understood these creatures. Did she really? Wendell watched carefully. When the last of the squirrels had passed, he began to follow them at a safe distance along the edge of the wood. They were heading somewhere. He thought he would like to see where.

·UPPER·FOREST·

"I don't understand it," Woodbine said, circling Brown Nut for the fourth time. "You seem perfectly all right. Not even a whisker bent out of shape."

"I *am* perfectly all right," Brown Nut replied. "I keep saying I am, and I am. Will you stop running around me and let me clean my feet? That cage I was in had been some other animal's den. Exactly what I could never figure out. Its scent is all over me—phew!"

"And you sound perfectly all right, too," Woodbine went on happily, while Laurel flicked her tail in amusement. "Just like your old self, sharp and snappy."

"I will get a lot snappier if you two don't stop fussing and allow me to tidy myself up," Brown Nut replied. "It's a dirty business being caught in an alien's nest. Bad food, bad water, and large, greasy paws making grabs from all sides. Uncomfortable, to say the least, though I was never in fear for my life."

"You weren't?"

"Oh no. The aliens actually thought they were giving me help, the poor things. They are quite sweet when you get to know them. The two you met are brother and sister."

"Brother and sister! How could you tell?"

"Scent, Woodbine. Scent. They smelled almost exactly alike."

Woodbine, who had never thought of being related to his sister by any more than a slight resemblance around the ears, opened his mouth to protest.

"Hush!" Laurel chittered suddenly. "Keep your voices low. Barker's patrol guards are everywhere in the forest."

"Barker's guards!" whispered Brown Nut in alarm. "What has been happening while I've been gone? I heard you speak of armies and gathering storms during our prayer for freedom in the invader's nest. (Which worked very well. Thank you both.) But I thought you were inventing things to persuade her to set me free."

"I wish we had been," Woodbine said. "The invader has no idea what is happening up here. We tried to warn her, but she couldn't understand."

"Understand what!" exclaimed Brown Nut.

At this, Woodbine and Laurel drew her away with them to a well-leafed nook, where they could hide and speak softly together. Laurel told of the big alien's surprise attack on the mink-tails who had followed Brown Nut's kidnappers through the forest, and of the meeting at Great Stump and the Elders' decision to call for an army.

Then Woodbine described the rise of Barker: how he had taken control of the troops and the Elders' minds, and brought the town to the brink of war.

"And now he calls me a traitor because I will not join the fight," Woodbine went on. "You see, I don't believe the aliens had any more idea of destroying our town than we had of driving them from theirs. They are rather like us in some respects, in their love of nests, for instance, and their incessant chatter. Though what their views are I can't begin to decipher. It would be interesting to study alien language and alien ways, to see how else one might live in Forest. Perhaps we mink-tails could learn a few things."

It was Brown Nut's turn to smile fondly at this. "Dear baby brother. You're more starry-eyed than ever. What could the poor aliens teach us? They are as flat and stupid as their land. For hours I sat in that wire cage while nothing, absolutely nothing, went on around me. A few senseless burbles and mutters, a sauntering to and fro, otherwise—"

"Well, if you knew more about them, you might have seen more," Woodbine couldn't help saying in an irritable voice.

A rattle of branches sounded from not far off, and the three fell instantly silent. They crouched under cover of the leaves as a mink-tail guard troop streamed by not ten feet from their hiding place.

"I have never seen such grim faces as those on these guards," Laurel breathed when they had passed. "We must be very careful, Woodbine, not to fall into their clutches."

Hearing this, Brown Nut gazed at her brother and Laurel with new admiration. "I had no idea you were taking such a risk in coming to find me in the aliens' den. How brave you both are!"

"Quiet! Something else is coming!" Laurel cried. They had barely ducked their heads when another large troop of guards rattled by, eyes combing the trees on all sides. "We have stayed here long enough!" she whispered. "It's time to move on."

"But where?" Brown Nut asked. "The whole forest is being patrolled, it seems."

"There's only one place we can go now," Woodbine said. "To Great Stump."

"Great Stump!" Brown Nut and Laurel looked at him in horror. "But that is now under Barker's command. We are sure to be arrested if we show ourselves there."

"That is true, but listen. The Elders are still in charge of Great Stump, though for how much longer we can only guess. We must talk with the old leaders before they grow too weak to help us."

"Well, I would be delighted to tell them about the humdrum lives of the aliens," Brown Nut said. "They certainly have no plot against our town, being far too caught up in their own flat ways."

"And I will tell them my observations of the invader," Woodbine said, "who never meant to invade our trees at all. She came to escape from her low world and had no idea that we lived here."

"The Elders might be interested to know how some aliens showed sorrow when one of their breed killed our squirrels, and took time to bury the dead in the honorable way," Laurel put in. "They are not all evil."

Woodbine nodded. "All right, then. I think we should try to sneak around by the pond. I know a little-used path there that is not so heavily guarded. Brown Nut, you go first as a decoy. If you are stopped, pretend you have just escaped from the aliens and give us time to get away."

Brown Nut bent her ears in agreement, but not before look-ing sharply at her brother. What had come over him? He sounded quite clear-headed.

The small group set off, their ears tuned to such sensitive frequencies that even faint beetle noises and the distant beat of wings were instantly detected.

Brown Nut led the way, avoiding the major branchways and running above the mink-tails' usual level of travel. Wood-bine followed, keeping his sister in sight. Laurel came last, a graceful, flitting tail. They ran so quickly and silently that the leaves hardly moved as they passed, and the birds went on singing undisturbed on their perches. Woodbine thought it strange that with all that was happening and threatening to happen in Forest, the town showed so little sign of trouble on its surface. Peacefully it flowed past his eyes, familiar and, all at once, very beautiful. Its colors were deep, its smells were rich, its sounds the comforting ones he'd heard all his life.

"Oh, Brown Nut!" Woodbine would have called, if they had not at that moment been in such danger. "Look, just look, at how lovely everything is!"

And she would have scoffed, probably, and told him it was about time he noticed where he lived, instead of thinking always of faraway places. Here Woodbine began to construct a theory (as he ran along) about how a squirrel longs for the places where he is not, and appreciates the place where he is only if it is suddenly in danger of being blasted out from under him. Hmm-mm, yes. How true. How very, very—

Branches thrashed on all sides of him. With incredible speed, Woodbine found himself surrounded by mink-tail guards.

"Halt! This way is closed."

"Oh, sorry. I didn't—"

"But who is this?" boomed a large, long-whiskered guard, lumbering forward for a closer look. The others in the troop perked up their ears.

"Aha! Woodbine. I thought I recognized you." The guard leered into his face, then motioned to two mink-tails behind him. "Here! This mink is wanted for questioning. It is Woodbine, the well-known traitor. Take him at once to the Supreme Commander's camp. But wait! Another spy has been caught."

Woodbine turned to see Laurel struggling with three guards in the tree just behind. In short order, they had subdued her and dragged her across to his branch.

"Name, please!"

"Laurel."

"You are charged with consorting with the cowardly traitor Woodbine. Do you deny it?"

"No."

"Take her away. Take them both away to the Supreme Commander's camp."

"Oh, Laurel, I'm so sorry!" Woodbine tried to whisper to her as they were jostled forward.

"Silence!" A back foot connected hard with his ribs. "The prisoners will not speak!"

They were marched away in double-time. Only when the last guard had gone, and the boughs of the trees had resumed their stately poses, did a dark eye peer out between the leaves. Brown Nut hopped forth and cocked her ears in the direction of the departed guard troop. With a small sniff, she began to follow in its path, moving as quietly and unnoticeably as a ray of light through the forest.

· ◆ ·

The afternoon was beginning to fade into the soft shades of early evening when Woodbine and Laurel arrived at the grove of pine trees that Barker had chosen for his camp. Never had they seen so many military troops in one place, so many guards marching and commanders issuing orders. The place was swirling with activity, and a continual rustle of pine boughs sounded on all sides. At the same time, a dull thunder rose off the forest floor from the heavy traffic of paws passing across it. Barker's troops had taken to the ground to practice their power swarms, which were so large and unwieldy that no tree would serve for training.

"Right flank, close! Left flank, swing!" The commanders' shouts echoed through the air. "Now attack straight ahead. Now drop back and swarm!"

The scene chilled Woodbine to the bone. When he turned to Laurel, he saw both fright and disgust in her eyes, and her long-ago words in the blackberry bush came again to him.

"What have we idiot mink-tails come to?" she had cried.

Well, what indeed.

"You! Prisoner! Into this hole." Woodbine was forced into a small, dark pine-tree den, sticky with sap. Behind him came Laurel, though there was hardly room for two. They crouched together flank to flank.

"I have never seen mink-tails act in such a brutal manner," Laurel whispered. "It's as if they enjoyed it. What will they do to us next?"

"I have no idea," Woodbine whispered back. "I suppose we will be kept here until Barker decides to question us."

This was such a grim prospect that the two were shortly reduced to silence. Then night fell, cutting off what little light there had been. In great discomfort, they managed to doze.

Long after midnight, when most in the camp had finally settled down, Woodbine was woken by a soft scratching noise. It seemed to come from the back of their tiny den, though there was no room there for so much as a cricket.

Scratch, scratch. Pause. Scratch, scratch.

"Someone is outside, scratching on the tree bark!" whispered Laurel, who had also been wakened. With some difficulty, she raised her back foot and rubbed it against the inner wall: Scratch, scratch.

Scratch, scratch! The message came back immediately.

"It's Brown Nut!" Woodbine hissed into Laurel's ear. Two mink-tail guards crouched not more than four feet away, near the entrance of their prison.

With a tremendous heave, Woodbine and Laurel managed to turn their poor wedged bodies around. Their mouths now nearly against the sticky back wall, they began a low chittering, deep in their chests.

They were answered! An instant later, Brown Nut's distinctive chirp came through the wood. She was certainly brave to have crept to the very center of Barker's command post. Woodbine felt a surge of admiration for her, but also fear. She must not be caught!

Her message to them was bleak. Escape was impossible at present. Their prison den was heavily guarded. A huge surprise attack against the aliens was scheduled for that morning.

Barker was taking no chances that his plans would be given away.

"I overheard a guard say that Barker plans to question you personally, when the attack is finished," Brown Nut whispered through the wall. "It won't be pleasant, I'm afraid. Try to be calm. I'll stay as near as I can."

"Please don't stay near! You'll just end up in here. And there's no room, even for us!" Woodbine hissed back. He was interrupted by the sharp voice of one of the guards.

"You, traitor! What is that muttering I hear?"

"Um . . . ahhh. . . " Woodbine and Laurel shrank together.

"Shut up in there, or we'll come and shut you up ourselves. We've been taught how to do it shockingly well, and can make things most uncomfortable for you. In fact, we would welcome the chance to try out our new education, ha, ha!"

Several minutes passed before Laurel dared to lean over and whisper in Woodbine's ear. What she said sent shivers down his spine:

"Woodbine, listen! Barker has become the most evil sort of dictator. He has stirred some dark impulse toward cruelty and power in the mink-tails. We must get to the Elders soon if we are to stop this horror. One thing becomes clearer with every passing hour: the town of Forest has been invaded by an enemy ten times more deadly than the aliens of the Lower Region!"

·LOWER·FOREST·

The upstairs hall was so dark when Amber stepped out into it that for a moment she lost her bearings. She reached for the wall to steady herself and nearly fell over when it wasn't there. Her broken arm jerked painfully in its sling.

"Ouch!"

"Amber? Is that you?"

"Yes!"

"Whew! I thought it was Mom," Wendell rasped from the doorway of his room. "I've been waiting here for hours. I was afraid I wouldn't wake up."

"Sh-sh! What's that clanking noise?"

They stood still for a long minute, listening. From their parents' room, a great whistling of air could be heard, punctuated at intervals by slurps and half-choked snorts.

"That's Dad," Wendell whispered. "I can't hear Mom."

"Come on, let's get going," Amber hissed, passing him on her way to the stairs. "No more talking until we get outside."

It was 5:10 A.M., and night was still very much in force, Amber noticed, as she closed the front door behind them. They walked away swiftly, down the center of the road. The streetlights made their shadows tall and thin. Above their heads the great trees of Forest spread black limbs, empty now of any squirrel activity.

With her good arm, Amber hitched the knapsack higher on her back. Inside were her wallet, the map of Randomville, her notebook, and the library's copy of *Woodland Animals and Their Habitats* by A. B. Spark. Her head was clear and cool this morning, and she'd remembered everything. The swelling from the gash on her chin had gone down. Now the bandage felt enormous.

"I must look like a war refugee," she joked to Wendell.

"More like someone who got blown up in a restaurant," he replied, gazing at her with such seriousness that she put her arm around his shoulders and gave him a hug.

"The bus leaves at five-thirty-two," she went on in businesslike tones. "It costs three-fifty for a round-trip ticket for one. It arrives at six-oh-three. We'll eat breakfast when we get there, in the station."

Amber stopped suddenly. "There's that clanking noise again," she whispered. "It seems to be following us."

Wendell glanced over his shoulder and shrugged. "Can I get a chocolate doughnut?" he asked.

He was quieter than usual, and Amber wondered if he was frightened. They had never been anywhere together alone.

"Sure," she said. "You can have anything that doesn't cost more than three-sixty-three. That's how much we'll have left over, each, after the bus fare. Including tax. And listen, you don't have to worry. I've taken the bus to Randomville before."

"Who's worried?" said Wendell.

They started off again. From a place low and behind them, Amber heard the eerie noise begin, too.

The sky was growing light when they reached the bus station, which was actually a small hut tucked next to the town gas station. Here, in contrast to the rest of Forest, a lively bustle was under way. The bus had already arrived and was fuming at the side of the road. People were beginning to climb on board.

"Two round-trip tickets for Randomville, please," Amber told the woman behind the ticket counter when their turn came in the line. She took out her wallet and put a five-dollar bill and two ones on the counter. The woman looked up.

"That'll get you to Randomville just fine," she said pleasantly. "It costs another seven dollars if you want to come back."

She looked at Wendell. "Isn't it a little early for you two to be out traveling?" she asked.

"I thought it was three-fifty for a round trip," Amber said loudly. "That's what my mother said when she left us off here."

"Well, she was mistaken. It's—"

"That's all right. We have enough." Amber handed seven more one-dollar bills to the woman, who punched a button and gave them their rickets.

"The bus is loading now," she said, pointing. "Are you sure everything is all right?"

They walked away fast and didn't talk until they were in their seats on the bus. Then Amber rolled her eyes.

"That was close," she whispered. "They must have misunderstood me when I called for information yesterday."

"You sounded great," Wendell whispered back. "I mean about Mom dropping us off. By the way, what's going to happen when Mom and Dad wake up and find us gone?"

"I left them a note. You and I are taking an early morning hike over Goodspeed Hill and will be back for lunch. If we can get back by then, we'll have it made. Otherwise, we'll have to call them. Mom would never forgive me if she had to start worrying about you, after all the time she's already put in on me."

Wendell smiled and sat back in his seat. "Speaking of lunch," he said, "I'm starved. I hope they have chocolate doughnuts at the place we're going for breakfast. Mom never lets me have them. Otherwise, I'll have to get a hot fudge sundae. Or chocolate cream pie. Or—"

"Um, Wendell?"

"What?"

"I hate to tell you this, but—"

"And milk," Wendell put in. "Don't worry, I'll get a big glass of milk, just as if Mom was here."

"I'm afraid," Amber said gently, "it's not a question of milk. I only have twenty-six cents left, and we'll need that for the pay phone if we have to call home."

Wendell positively beamed at this. He reached up and put his arm around his sister's shoulders, though he almost had to stand up to reach them.

"That's okay, Amber," he said. "You don't have to worry. I'll pay for breakfast, and you can have anything you want. Absolutely anything!"

Wendell really did stand up now, and shoved a hand into his pocket. There was a tremendous rattle and clank.

"I brought my own money," he said proudly.

"Good grief! That's what that noise was. How much did you bring?"

"Well, all of it, actually. Sixty-five dollars and sixty-eight cents. I made some of it, and sometimes Dad gives me his change."

"Sixty-five dollars!" Amber yelled. For the first time she noticed how Wendell's pants rode dangerously low on his hips; how his legs had a peculiar lamb chop–ish look—skinny in the shank, fat around the pockets.

"I thought if there was an emergency, then we might need it," Wendell said. "And now there *is* an emergency!" He sat down with a modest jingle.

"Wendell Padgett, you are fantastic!" cried Amber.

"Thank you."

"That is the best thinking you've ever done!"

"I know." Wendell blushed with pleasure.

"We'll be able to eat the most incredible breakfast of all time! And still have tons of money left over! In fact," said Amber, "we'd better eat a big breakfast or you're never going to make it to Professor Spark's house. We need to unload you a little, from the look of those pants."

"Oh, I don't mind," Wendell said happily. "I just hang on to my belt and yank it up every once in a while."

They ate the most incredible breakfast of all time. Wendell had chocolate frosted doughnuts and honey-dip doughnuts, scrambled eggs and bacon, hot chocolate and hash brown potatoes and cream cheese and bagels. He ordered a hot fudge sundae for dessert. Amber had three different kinds of french toast and raspberry maple syrup, orange juice and sausages and blueberry muffins, and then went on to strawberry pie. Even with two cracked teeth, it tasted delicious.

Afterward, Wendell's pants stayed up much better, and they were able to make fast time walking through the city. A lot of people were up by this hour, and the streets were filled with cars. Amber paid attention to traffic lights, and signposts, and never once had to take out the map. She'd memorized their route the night before and knew exactly where they were at every corner.

"Why Mom ever bothers to worry about you, I don't know," Wendell said, puffing along behind. "They could probably ship you blindfolded to the moon, and you'd know exactly where you were in thirty seconds."

"And in fact here we are!" Amber announced, halting in front of a rather shabby brick apartment house.

"Are you sure?" Wendell asked. "It doesn't look like the kind of place an important professor would live, especially one that studies woodland habitats. There's not a tree or bush on this whole block."

Amber did not have time to reply, for suddenly the front door of the apartment house flew open and a white-haired woman appeared, clutching the ends of several leashes.

"Come along! Come along, dear friends and neighbors! We're late this morning. Trot out. Trot out," the woman cried. Then down the front steps in a waterfall of legs came dogs of various shapes and sizes. The onslaught nearly knocked Wendell and Amber over.

"So sorry!" cried the woman as she was dragged by. "Morning walk, you know! Been cooped up all night. Are you looking for anyone? Might I be of some help?"

The dog-walker pulled on the leashes and turned toward the children. She was hardly taller than Wendell and did not look equal to her high-spirited troop.

"Well, actually, yes," said Amber. "Could you tell us if Professor Spark lives in this building? Professor A. B. Spark, the man who studies forests? We've come to see him about a very urgent matter."

The white-haired woman smiled and nodded. Then, finding herself being dragged away down the sidewalk, she shouted to them over her shoulder.

"Yes! I know Professor Spark. Unfortunately, he has just gone out! But he'll be back shortly, so if you just take a seat on the steps, you'll be sure not to miss him!"

"Oh, thank you!" cried Amber, and she and Wendell sat down on the apartment house steps.

Twenty minutes later, the professor had not returned when the old lady careened back up the sidewalk, in no better control of her pack than before.

"Hello! Here you still are, I see!" she cried as she passed them going up the steps. "You might as well come in and wait. I know Professor Spark's apartment and will be heading in that direction. Here is his dog, India, in fact!—acquired during the professor's trip to study the amazing rain forests of that place. She is half hyena, I believe—a sweet thing, don't you think? The other dogs belong to the neighbors. It is my duty to walk them in the mornings. Evenings fall to someone else."

During this rather breathless speech, Amber and Wendell trailed the white-haired lady up stairs and along various corridors as she opened doors and pushed selected dogs inside, and quickly shut the doors again. At last only the professor's India was left. She was not really sweet-looking at all but scant-haired and thickset, with the most vicious set of choppers Amber and Wendell had ever seen on a dog.

"Here we are!" announced their guide, opening another door. "Professor Spark's own sorry habitat. He is underpaid, you see. Writing books is a poor man's trade. If only the woodland animals he studies could see the beastly conditions under which he is forced to live, they would offer him shelter in their own nests, no doubt.

"Or rather," the tiny woman continued, coming about suddenly to face the children, "they would offer *her* shelter. For I am, of course, Professor A. B. Spark. Professor Anna Belle Spark, that is, and most curious to know what brings you to my door."

• ♦ •

"I apologize for playing that silly trick on you," the professor chuckled a few minutes later, after introductions were finished and the three of them were seated in her worn living room.

"You fooled us all right," Amber said with a grin. "We never for a minute guessed who you were." Wendell shook his head.

Professor Spark chuckled again and reached out to pat India. "It's a small revenge I extract whenever the opportunity arises. How would you like to be constantly mistaken for a man? And not just any man, mind you, but a large-headed, hairy-chested one, with full beard and biceps. The trouble is misconception, of course. People see these brawny types on the television studying polar bears inside the Arctic Circle, or tracking snow leopards through the wilds of Tibet, and they think all wildlife experts should look that way. You can imagine the wear and tear on those of us who don't fit the mold."

"But isn't it hard for you, getting around in forests and across rough terrain?" Amber asked. "You are so small, smaller than I am, even. And quite a lot older. What if you had to fight off a lion?"

"You are speaking of brute strength, I suppose," Professor Spark said with a sniff. "Pish-tosh, brute strength! It has little to do with survival in the wilds. What modern-day woodland professional would be so stupid as to put herself in a position where brute strength alone could save her? We have brains, my dear." The professor touched her forehead. "It is our great invention, we *Homo sapiens*. Young or old, female or other, we think our way around trouble and through forests of every sort."

Amber gave a deep sigh when she heard this. It made her feel more confident, somehow. And even Wendell sat up and looked interested.

"Well, we have run into a sort of trouble we can't think around," he said bluntly. "That's why we're here."

Professor Spark glanced at her watch. "I have fifteen minutes before classes start," she said. "I teach at the university, you know, to keep out of the poorhouse. If you could give me some idea of your situation before—"

Amber and Wendell did not wait for her to finish. They leapt at the opening and began at once to tell her about the amazing squirrels of Forest, about their trees and ancient pathways, their strange tails and eyes, their silver-haired raft of leaders, their chittery language, their wonderful songs.

"The thing is that no one had ever bothered to look up before," Amber explained. "I suppose these squirrels were always there, but no one ever noticed."

"And now our dad and Chief Teckstar have organized a search-and-destroy mission. For this morning!" Wendell said.

"They are making a terrible mistake," Amber added angrily. "The squirrels only meant to protect themselves, not hurt us."

"Although they did hurt us," Wendell said, pointing to Amber's broken arm and her chin. "You can see how everything got started."

"What I see," said the professor, nodding sympathetically, "is another case of misconception. Squirrels happen to be among my favorite species in the woodland world. People have such queer ideas about them. Vermin they are called, when they are honest, hardworking mammals, the same as you and me. Diseased, people say, infested, teeming, inbred: if squirrels could talk, they would no doubt protest these unfair views of them and their culture."

"But they *can* talk!" cried Amber and Wendell together.

"At least, our squirrels can," Amber said.

"But not in our language," Wendell added.

"I see that I must take action at once!" Professor Spark exclaimed, rising to her feet. "These extraordinary creatures must be saved from extinction. What a loss to the world if their gentle breed were ended, if they went without a murmur to history's silent grave, if they—"

"Wait a minute, Professor Spark." Wendell held up his hand to get her attention. "Excuse me, but I think you have caught a case of misconception yourself. These squirrels aren't about to go anywhere without a murmur. We've seen them in action, so we should know. I wouldn't really call them a gentle breed, either, since they are training right now to fight a war if they have to."

"Training!" The professor gazed at him in surprise.

"War!" said Amber. "What on earth do you mean?"

"I saw them," Wendell said. "In the forest yesterday, and up by the big apple farms. While you were resting, Amber, I heard a lot of rustling. So I went out and did some more spying. The squirrels have organized themselves into armies. They have captains and lieutenants and have learned to march in swarms through the trees. In one place, I saw them practicing what looked like an attack."

Professor Spark's eyes shifted uneasily.

"This is very unusual," she said. "I don't like the sound of it at all. If your squirrels have half the brain you say they do, we may be in for a very nasty time."

"I don't understand it!" exclaimed Amber. "These squirrels were never vicious. They were playful and peaceful, and curious in a good-natured way."

"Well, something's happened to them," Wendell said. "They've changed."

"And we had better get moving if we're to head off a fight," Professor Spark declared. "The first thing to do, if I may suggest it, is to stop your father's hunting party. Hmm, what time is it? Good heavens, nearly nine o'clock! I will telephone and cancel my classes. I have a car in the garage in the basement. We'll leave immediately for the town of Forest! I hope it isn't already too late."

Not more than five minutes later, they were out the door, winding down corridors and stairs to the basement.

"Professor Spark, wait! India is following us," Amber

called. "Shall I take her back and put her in your apartment?"

"Certainly not!" the professor replied, with a wave of her tiny hand. "India comes on all my expeditions. She may not look it, adorable little thing, but she's an expert herself on wildlife of every sort!"

"In this case, I can certainly believe it," Amber murmured to Wendell as India and her terrifying mouthful of teeth caught up and passed them going down the stairs.

·UPPER·FOREST·

Night's black wings were just beginning to fold away when the first small group of mink-tails stirred in Barker's camp. These were the morning guards, those scheduled to relieve the night patrol of watch duty. They pulled themselves sleepily from their makeshift nests and trundled along tree limbs to the lookout points.

"Ho, Woodburn! Treebud reporting for work."

"Ho, Treebud, am I glad to see you! This night watch business is for the birds."

"I know. I have a hard enough time staying awake during the day."

"Sh-sh! Not so loud. the Supreme Commander has big ears. One small complaint, and wham! You're landed in the hole."

"You're telling me! My sister is in solitary confinement right now—for eating an acorn."

"What? That's crazy!"

"The orders are, no eating during boundary patrol checks."

"What does Barker think we are—reptiles? We need to eat more than once a day."

"Sh-sh! Not so loud. There are spies everywhere. You can't trust your own mother."

"To tell you the truth, I'm not sure I do trust her."

"Sh-sh-sh!"

From their cramped quarters, Woodbine and Laurel listened glumly to this conversation between two guards stationed in front of their tree cell. The situation in Forest was worsening by the hour. Meanwhile, they sat helpless, hardly able to move a muscle. Their bodies were stiff after a long night crouched in the same position. Their minds were fogged with exhaustion and worry.

Outside, as the light grew stronger, the sounds of armies assembling rose around them. They heard the sharp barks of the commander guards ordering troops into formation. They heard the thunder of paws as hordes of soldier minks swept across the forest floor beneath them. They heard the squeaks of soldiers being punished for some blunder, and the screeching protests of birds whose feeding territories were being disturbed. From overhead came a rattle of branches as more troops arranged themselves for aerial attack on the enemy.

"Where is Brown Nut?" Woodbine dared to whisper once, in a voice barely audible above the hubbub outside. Since there was no possible answer to this, Laurel merely lowered her head and thought longingly of blackberry bushes she had known in her day.

Soon to the prisoners' ears came the unmistakable noises of mass departure. Before long the thundering troops were gone, and such a silence settled over the place that the two were encouraged to creep forward and peek out their hole.

"Halt! Get back there!"

A guard blocked the entrance. Woodbine and Laurel were shoved violently back inside.

"Any trouble with the prisoners, Birch Bark?" a harsh voice inquired.

"None, Treebud. They are weaklings without a spark of courage. I need no help. If you'd like to take a break, I'll look after them for a few minutes."

"Nice of you. Perhaps I will go off for a bit of breakfast now that the troops have left. Can I bring you anything?"

"No, but you can take over for me when you get back."

"Agreed." There was a bustle of retreating paws. Then quiet.

"You! Cowards! Move farther back. And no talking." The cruel shadow of the guard fell over Woodbine and Laurel in their hole. They squeaked in terror and cringed together like the most pitiful of cowards. Never had they been so miserable. Never had the world seemed so dreadful. It is all very well to speak of courage when you are safe, but when you are crushed for hours in a hot, dark hole and surrounded by guards who boast of their talent for torture—forget it. With tear-filled eyes, the prisoners gazed up into the brutal, evil, angry face of . . .

"Brown Nut! What are you—"

"Sh-sh! Do you want me to get caught? . . . Take that, you mink-tailed rat!" Brown Nut's foot materialized suddenly in front of Woodbine's nose, halting just before it struck. "Let that be a lesson to you to keep away from the light!"

A second later her anxious face looked in at them. "Are you all right? Good. Wait for my signal. We're going to make a run for it."

She vanished again and became the loathsome shadow of the guard.

In the moments that followed, Woodbine and Laurel tried frantically to untangle their legs, and to rub their paws to get the blood moving through them again. They had been cramped for so long that they were afraid they had lost the ability to run. There was not much time to worry, though. Brown Nut's tail flicked into the opening, a sign that they must prepare for flight.

An instant later the tail snapped out of sight as Brown Nut leapt for a branch below. Woodbine and Laurel appeared in the entrance, blinking in the bright daylight. Then they also sprang for the branch, and all three spiraled headlong down a pine tree's trunk. Across open ground they fled, into a clump of bushes, through a thicket of young scrub trees, and up another pine tree, where they hid out briefly, their eyes watching the branches on all sides.

They sped off again, following Brown Nut. And though their escape was quickly discovered, and a search party formed, it posed no danger. The three mink-tails soon slipped out of sight and were lost in Upper Forest's green swirl of leaves.

◆ ◆ ◆

From the Supreme Commander's headquarters, a half-rotted pine tree at the center of his camp:

"Well? What of the prisoners?"

"We regret to report, sir, that their escape has been successful. They have fled into the Third Quadrant."

"This news does not please me. Have the responsible guards been punished?"

"Yes, Supreme Commander, sir. The guard Treebud is on his way to the swamp now, for drowning. The second guard was an impostor. She tricked Treebud into taking a break for breakfast. Then she helped the prisoners escape and went with them."

"Who is this traitor? Have you a name?"

"Brown Nut, sir. The prisoner's sister."

"Brown Nut! I am sorry to hear it. She has survived the aliens, then, and returned to undermine our cause. Send five hundred soldier minks to search the Third Quadrant immediately. All three traitors must be caught! I fear they will try to make their way to the Elders. Triple our security forces around Great Stump."

"Yes, Supreme Commander, sir. But I will have to order some troops back from the front to make up that number. Every male, female, and kit is involved in our attack on the aliens this morning."

"Well, do it, idiot!"

"Yes sir. Here are three messenger minks from the front, Supreme Commander. They come with information about the attack."

"Speak up, fools! How goes our glorious fight?"

"Very well, sir."

"Excellently, sir."

"Brilliantly, sir!"

"Well? Go on!"

"The apple orchards north of town are being destroyed, sir, according to plan. The fruit is being devoured and the trees damaged."

"Good! Many aliens depend on these apples for their livelihood."

"Our attack on the aliens' communication system is going well, too, sir. Many lines along their paths have been bitten through or clawed."

"Good work! The aliens will be forced outside their box nests to communicate, which they will not like. Especially since our troops are there, waiting to swoop down!"

"The magic juice is our next target, sir."

"All *right*! We have them by the throat! When these actions are completed, send our troops to the Lower Region pathways to cut off incoming aid. The aliens must be made to taste fear on their tongues. Only then will they go forever from our town."

"Ahem! Supreme Commander, sir. I must report also, with great sadness, the death in battle of five mink-tail squirrels in the First Quadrant, five more in the Second, and fifteen in the Fourth, where a band of aliens is roaming with fire weapons."

"Excellent! We have hardly been injured at all! What are a mere twenty-five minks subtracted from the thousands in our power swarms? It will make no difference to our battle plan at all!"

"Yes, sir. I suppose not, sir. Some of them were children."

"Well, we have plenty more to take their places! Order all swarms to the Fourth Quadrant immediately to destroy this alien band. Then proceed with the magic juice attacks. And now please leave me. I must begin to make plans for our victory celebration. Shall we have fireworks? The aliens' weapons will be ours for the taking!"

· ◆ ·

The sun was about halfway up the sky when Woodbine, Laurel, and Brown Nut reached the majestic beeches that grew around Great Stump. So tall and thick-leaved were these trees that the clearing surrounding the stump was still in shadow, though the morning was well advanced.

"We must move quickly," Brown Nut told the others. "The shade gives us cover to make our approach. An hour from now the ground will be bright with sunlight. Also, Barker is too smart not to know where we are headed. He will certainly have ordered more troops to Great Stump to keep us away. At the moment, the Elders are lightly guarded, it appears."

"But even if we do get in, will the Elders agree to listen to us?" Laurel whispered anxiously. "They may simply call the guards and order us dragged off."

"That is true, but we must take the risk," Woodbine answered. "Our ancient leaders are the only ones with power enough to challenge Barker."

"And if the Elders are persuaded against Barker, will Forest's mink-tails follow?" Laurel asked. "Barker has raised in their blood a hunger for battle. Perhaps the Elders' power is already gone."

"There is no way to tell," Brown Nut said, "unless we try. And we must try immediately, or lose our advantage."

Not long after, the mink-tails separated and crept to hiding places around the clearing. Then, taking their cue from Woodbine, they each set out toward the stump, using the sort of scamper-and-halt, scuttle-and-freeze technique that is the trademark of all squirrels crossing open ground. At first there was no movement anywhere, and it seemed that the stump guards might be asleep at their posts, or off eating a late breakfast. The three came quite close to Great Stump, close enough to see the jagged hole in its crown that led down to the Elders' chambers below.

But then, suddenly, the game was up. As if some warning system had been tripped (and perhaps it had), Woodbine found himself leapt upon by guards on the stump's eastern flank. At the same moment Laurel, though she dodged brilliantly, was attacked and brought down on the west side. Brown Nut, to the south, did not even bother to put up a fight. She tried, true to form, to bluster her way through.

"Please! I am the kidnapped Brown Nut, recently released by the aliens," Woodbine heard her say to the guards in outraged tones.

"Oh, sure! Brown Nut! Ha, ha. She is long dead in the aliens' clutches." Several guards chuckled together.

"I am not dead! I come with a message from the aliens," said Brown Nut, becoming more inventive. "Please escort me to the Elders at once. My companions and I have top-secret information that must reach their ears."

"Top-secret information. Ha, ha, ha, ha. Barker would love this. Take her away, Woodside."

Still Brown Nut would not give up. She shook off her captors and narrowed her eyes.

"My message is not for Supreme Commander Barker but for our wise leaders," she spat out. "I warn you, guards, if the Elders do not receive this message, they will be extremely angry. It is an answer to a message they sent yesterday, in utmost secrecy, to the Lower Region. Do you think the Elders are Barker's servants? Of course not! They report to no one and take action of their own!"

The guards were thrown into spluttering confusion by this statement, which was such a complete lie that Woodbine's paws began to sweat.

"Did the Elders send a message to the Lower Region?" the guards asked one another.

"I don't know."

"Maybe this mink-tail is telling the truth."

"Maybe she is lying."

"We don't want to anger the Elders."

"We don't want to upset Barker, either."

"So take them to the Elders and see what happens. What harm could it do?"

"I dunno."

"Sure, take them."

"But we have orders from the Supreme Commander not to allow anyone . . ."

This last remark was drowned out, luckily, by the guards urging their captives forward into the stump's entrance. A few moments later, Brown Nut, Woodbine, and Laurel found themselves being escorted along a tunnel that plunged almost straight down into the ground.

It was an ancient tunnel, one that the young mink-tails had only heard tell of in stories. In the old, old days, Great Stump had been a living tree, a tremendous beech that towered over all the other trees around it. At that time mink-tail leaders had craved height, and the beech became a natural gathering place for them. Only as the years went on, and the great tree had aged and lost branches, decayed, and turned hollow, had the gathering place gradually settled groundward. Then a windstorm had knocked the beech over altogether, and the wise ones' chamber had moved underground.

The tunnel followed the track of the old tree's giant tap root and ended deep in the earth at the Elders' vast ceremonial chamber. Now, as Woodbine was hustled toward this fabulous place, he recalled the story of the brilliant mink-tail builder Wolfeye, who had conceived and designed the chamber, and then, through sheer force of will (a will that carried on even after his death), persuaded generations of squirrels to labor underground for a hundred years. A hundred years! It seemed impossible. Woodbine could not imagine spending even a week in this dark and gritty world. Mink-tails were not underground hibernators, like some in the squirrel family.

"Halt! Please proceed slowly. The chamber is just ahead," a guard warned.

Then they were passing into a hall whose ceiling curved pale and high over their heads, and whose walls glowed dimly from some luminous mineral embedded in them. The feeling the room gave was of an immense and peaceful center. It was as if they had come inside a moon and were gazing out through its shining skin.

"Amazing!" breathed Laurel.

"Incredible!" gasped Woodbine.

"There they are," Brown Nut said in her sensible, unflappable way. "The Elders. Don't forget to bow."

And there they were indeed, a rather gloomy-looking group of silver-haired leaders perched on a raised platform at one end of the chamber. As the little troop of visitors approached, the Elders' heads came up, one by one, and their tails rose here and there to attention. They looked like a bleary-eyed, many-headed creature rousing itself after a long nap. As they more or less were, Woodbine later found out, for so many days had passed since they had last been consulted that their minds had begun to dim.

"Barker? Is that you?" the Elders called out together, peering and squinting at the oncoming forms. This was such a pathetic cry to hear from the once-powerful protectors of Forest's ancient realm that Woodbine felt his heart sink into his stomach. Brown Nut, however, wasted no time on emotion.

"Honorable lords and ladies," she began. "We are here to report terrible happenings in Forest. May we come closer and speak to you in private?"

The Elders nodded groggily and drew back on their platform to make room. Terrible happenings? Where was Supreme Commander Barker? He handled these things.

"But it's about Barker that we've come to see you," Woodbine told the many heads. "Do you know that the mink-tails are at war? We are attacking the aliens at this very moment."

The Elders blinked in surprise at this information. But they had no time to answer because just then the sound of running feet echoed from the tunnel, and a breathless group of guards burst into the great chamber. Without stopping to bow, they rushed directly for the Elders' platform.

"Arrest these spies at once!" a voice barked out behind the guards. "Remove them from the chamber! Whoever let them in will pay in blood."

"Barker!" squeaked Laurel, shrinking back in fright.

In seconds the three young mink-tails were gripped by the guards, who began to drag them away. The Elders drew aside from this scuffle with distaste. They were not used to violence of any sort, but to see it here, in the great ceremonial hall, well, it was disrespectful. No—more than that—it was shocking! Actually, it was an outrage, and should be stopped before it went any further!

"Guards! Release the visitors!" the Elders commanded. "They came to speak to us about affairs of state. We are curious to hear what they have to say."

The guards stopped in confusion and looked over at Barker. What should they do now?

"Guards! Take the cowards away!" the Supreme Commander ordered. "Our wise Elders do not understand. The affairs of Forest have grown too complicated for their fine old heads!"

"Oh no they haven't!" the Elders shouted back angrily. "We begin to see quite clearly what is happening in our land. Guards! The visitors are ordered to stay!"

At this, Barker himself stepped with a slippery movement onto the Elders' platform. He bowed deeply to the wrathful leaders and softened his voice.

"Your majesties, I beg your pardon," he said, in such oily tones that Woodbine, standing nearby, bristled. "I only wanted to protect you from unpleasantness. These youngsters are traitors with nothing to say but lies."

"We Elders will be the judge of that," the Elders rumbled back. "Guards! Remove your grip from our visitors."

"Guards! Take them away!" thundered Barker.

The guards' heads swung back and forth. They did not

know whom to believe, or whom to obey. They stood still, holding fast to Laurel, Woodbine, and Brown Nut while they tried to make up their minds. The sight of this indecision sent Barker into a rage.

"Idiots!" he screamed. "I am Supreme Commander. Listen to me, not these old fur balls. They are weak and have no bite."

At the mention of fur balls, Woodbine's tail shot straight up in the air. Until this moment, he had been submitting quietly to the guards' grip. Now a terrible fury flashed through him. Before he could stop himself, he wrenched free and lunged at Barker. Snap! He sunk his teeth deep into Barker's ratty tail. Oh, it felt so good!

There was a shriek of pain. Several guards sprang forward to tear the two apart. This was a most fortunate turn of events. The Elders, seeing Barker in the hands of the guards, promptly ordered them to take the traitor away. And the guards, shocked back to their old loyalties, promptly did as they were told. In a second the crisis was over.

"Let me go!" Barker cried as they dragged him off. "It's a trick! I have done nothing—only served the mink-tails faithfully!"

The Elders turned their backs. Their minds had become crystal-sharp. They saw all that they had missed during the past days. They came forward and congratulated Woodbine on his timely bite, "though we do not as a rule approve of this kind of activity," they added hastily.

"Woodbine doesn't, either," Brown Nut assured them, with a stern look at her brother. "He usually has better control of himself."

Woodbine nodded sheepishly and silently vowed to keep a short leash on himself in the future. He was still not sure how it had happened. He was normally such a shy, retiring squirrel.

"And now tell us quickly about this war!" the Elders demanded. "What fools we have been. We may all be wiped out. Is it possible to call back our troops before any more damage is done?"

"I am afraid it may already be too late," Brown Nut said. "I've been speaking just now to Barker's guards. Our power swarms are at this very minute closing in on a band of aliens with weapons not far from here. Their orders are to destroy them."

"Destroy them! But I thought we were only going after their living systems!" Woodbine said in alarm. "We were never supposed to actually kill the aliens."

"These aliens have been killing soldier minks in the Fourth Quadrant," Brown Nut said, "so there is deep feeling against them."

The Elders sighed and shook their many heads. "What fools we were!" they moaned again. "Come. Let us go quickly to the Fourth Quadrant. We must all pray that the battle has not yet begun!"

·LOWER·FOREST·

The terrible heat that had plagued Forest for the better part of two weeks was on the rise again as Amber, Wendell, and Professor Spark sped along toward town in the professor's old car. The hayfields on either side of the road were wilting in the sun. An odor of scorched tar came in through the windows, which were wide open and streaming wind.

"Whew!" shouted the professor above the blow. "This is worse than India! No, no, not you, sweetie," she added, patting the dog, which had lunged to its feet in the front seat. Amber, who was occupying the front seat, too, inched closer to the door.

"Take a left at the next corner," she called across to the professor. "Apple Farm Road. It heads right into town. I think we should stop at the firehouse first, to find out if the search-and-destroyers have left, and where they might have gone."

"Good idea," answered the professor. She gave Amber an admiring glance. "You certainly are a person who steps up and takes charge."

Amber blushed with pleasure at this and was trying to think of a humble-sounding reply when Wendell let out a squawk in the backseat. The professor jammed on the brakes.

"Look!" Wendell shrieked, pointing out the car window. "Something's happened to the apple trees!"

"Good grief! They've been torn to shreds!" cried Amber. "For miles in every direction! And where are all the apples? I can't see a single one."

"I was afraid of this," said Professor Spark, putting her shrimp-size foot to the gas pedal again. "It looks as if the squirrels have already made an attack. Very bad, my dears. Very dangerous. Hang on to your hatpins—I'm picking up the tempo a bit."

With this she stamped the car's gas pedal to the floor, and the car shot ahead like a missile. The landscape blurred. The wind beat at their faces. It was impossible to see or hear or say anything for several minutes. They arrived at the firehouse with a screech of tires and leapt out on the sidewalk.

Only then, looking around, did they notice something odd about the town. It was deathly quiet. There were no cars in the street, or people. There were no children playing in yards, no baby carriages parked in the shade or water sprinklers on the lawns. Many wires were down along the road. In a house across the way, Amber saw a face surface at a window and draw away.

"This is a town under siege if ever I saw one," Professor Spark declared. "I'm afraid our squirrels are turning more vicious by the hour."

"But that's impossible!" cried Amber. "It's all a terrible

mistake. These squirrels are peaceful, civilized creatures. This can't be happening!"

Even as she spoke, however, a strange, low rustle started in the distance. It might have been wind rushing toward them through the trees—if the day had been stormy; or the wash of surf on a rocky shore—if Forest had been near the ocean. Wendell turned pale. He grabbed Amber by the hand.

"Squirrels!" he bellowed, and pulled her toward the firehouse. "Come inside, quick! They move like lightning."

They scrambled for the big doors, which flew open as they approached, and closed down so fast behind them that Professor Spark almost lost India, and India very nearly parted with her tail.

And then, from the roof, came such a scrabble of small feet that no one dared move for several minutes. Amber and Wendell stood gazing at the rafters amid a quaking group of volunteer firemen. Professor Spark moved to a window and narrowed her eyes.

"Amazing!" she exclaimed when the hordes had passed. "I've never seen anything like this in all my years of research. Amber, you are quite right about these squirrels. They have achieved a level of organization far beyond others of their species. Unfortunately, it is being used for destructive purposes at the moment. Don't look so surprised, my dear. It's in the nature of the beast."

"But these squirrels are not beasts!" Amber protested.

"Oh, pish-tosh, we are all of us beasts," the professor replied lightly. "The trouble comes when we try to pretend that we're not. And that is why we must act quickly," she went on. "The hunting party must be found and stopped before things get any worse. We don't want a full-scale war on our hands. Does anyone know where the men have gone?"

After a brief discussion with several firemen, she nodded and beckoned to Amber and Wendell.

"India and I are going into the forest," she said. "Will you come with us? It's dangerous, I'm afraid, but your knowledge of the area would be a great help."

"Of course we'll come!" Amber said. "We couldn't stand to be left behind now." Wendell was already emptying the change from his pockets. He tucked in his shirt, cinched in his belt, and double-knotted his shoelaces.

"Ready for action," he announced grimly. "I'm a beast, and I know it. I've got my slingshot this time. If anything tries to attack us, I'm shooting it between the eyes!"

"Wendell," said Amber, "remember, these are our friends the squirrels you're talking about. They are not savages."

"And then I'm shooting them *through* the eyes . . ."

"Wendell, please!"

". . . and through the ears and nose and neck and guts, and if that doesn't stop them, I'm . . ."

"Wendell, that is horrible!"

". . . I'm taking out my jackknife and skinning them from head to foot like the trappers do for squirrel coats. And then I'm chopping up the meat into little bits and putting it in a pot and . . ."

"Wendell!"

Amber grabbed him by the collar before he could say any more, and dragged him out the firehouse door, following Professor Spark.

Bam! Bam! Bam! Zing! Bam!

From a clearing surrounded by giant beech trees some-where in the middle of the forest, the sound of shots rico-cheting through branches rang out. A shower of leaves drifted earthward as the figures of two hunters stepped from the bushes below.

"Did you see one, Padgett?"

"Naw. Just a bunch of scared birds. Come on, Teckstar. Let's sit down on this stump and wait for the others to catch up. We've gotten a little ahead."

"Sure. Okay. Where are all these supposedly rabid squirrels, anyway? I haven't seen one."

"They're here. Hiding out, probably. Look at these enor-mous trees! I guess I've never been so far into the forest be-fore."

"Me either."

"I mean, I knew the place was old, but wow! This stump should be in a museum. What a monster. I wonder if the Natural History Museum in Randomville would be inter-ested? They could bring a backhoe in here and dig it up and use it for an exhibit. The kids would love it. . . . Um, what's that noise?"

"That rustling, you mean?"

"Sounds like wind coming toward us."

"Except there isn't any wind. It's flat calm."

"Hey, Teckstar. Have you ever been to the beach?"

"One time. When I was a kid."

"Well, doesn't this sound sort of like . . ."

"Waves! Rolling in to shore."

"That's what I was thinking. Except we're not there."

"Where?"

"At the beach! So it can't be waves!"

"Well, what is it, then? It's getting closer."

"Um . . . "

"Listen, Padgett. It's getting louder. I don't like this at all. Let's start back and see where the others are. We should keep together in case anything . . ."

"Ah . . ."

"What is that up there?"

"Ah . . ."

"Squirrels! Lord save us, a huge swarm of squirrels! There must be thousands! No, millions!"

"Teckstar, they're moving like lightning!"

"I've never seen anything like this in my life!"

BAM! Bam. Bam.

BLAST! BAM!

"Run, Padgett! It's no good trying to shoot them. There're too many. Run! Help! They're closing in!"

"Help! Help!"

"Help! Help! Oh, he . . . . . lp!"

• ◆ •

Professor Spark paused under a tree and held up her hand.

"Wait a minute," she said. "I think India heard something."

Wendell and Amber stopped walking and listened to the forest noises around them. Off to their right, India had come to a halt, ears cocked. A series of little pops went off in the distance.

"Gunshots!" exclaimed Amber.

"I heard them, too," Wendell said. "They seemed to come from over there." He pointed through the trees, away to the left.

"Beyond the pond," Amber said. "Come on!"

They marched along in silence, single file. India trotted with them, a shadowy form to one side. Every once in a while she would pause and lift her ears. Then she moved on again, sniffing as she went. Amber noticed that the professor never took her eyes off the dog for long, and when India began to trot faster, she lengthened her own strides.

"She's onto something. She's smelled something, I'm sure," the professor said.

They increased their pace to keep up. A rumble of gunshots broke out in front of them, much nearer. The forest was sweltering. Amber pushed her damp hair off her forehead. Wendell's face had turned a tropical pink.

"I'm just not a forest person, okay?" he snapped when Amber asked him if he felt all right. "Every time I'm in the forest, something bad happens. I'd rather be home watching TV, if you really want to know."

"TV!" exclaimed Professor Spark. "That feeble substitute for adventure? I'd rather sit home with the flu!"

Amber smiled. She'd been watching the older woman. Professor Spark might not understand television, but when it came to forests, she was in a class by herself. Cool and confident, she moved between the trees as if she were among friends in a place she knew well. Her white hair was slicked back under a camouflage-colored scarf. Her tiny feet skimmed through the brush. She knew the names of everything, plants, animals, and rocks, and pointed them out as they sped along. A compass was strung on a thong around her neck. At intervals she stopped to check their position. Amber had never thought about positions before. She made a mental note to get a compass for herself.

It was during one of the professor's halts that Amber noticed something strange about India. The dog was standing stiffly in a clearing about fifteen yards away, hackles raised. As Amber watched, its thick hyena lips curled back in a snarl.

"Look! India sees something!" she cried. Immediately the sound of cracking underbrush reached their ears. Not more than ten seconds later, the hunting party stormed down on them, at least twenty men running at top speed through the woods with their guns.

"Mad squirrels! Go back! Back!" some of the hunters shouted. Others tried to speak as they raced by, but couldn't for lack of breath.

"Dad!" cried Wendell, catching sight of his father. His shout seemed to bring the whole group up short. They spun around with wild eyes.

"Wendell! Amber!" Mr. Padgett called. "What are you doing here? Run back! The squirrels are right behind us!"

Even as he shouted, however, the rustling that everyone knew by now rose out of the woods behind him. At the same time, more rustling sounded to the right of the hunting party, and still more from the left, and it became clear that they were all surrounded. There was nowhere left for anyone to run.

Chief Teckstar took charge immediately. Fast-moving fires were his specialty.

"All right, men, prepare to dig in and fight!" the big fireman ordered. "There's not a moment to lose. Women and children to the middle. Marksmen, form a circle around them. Guns set! Ammunition handy!"

Professor Spark sprang forward with a cry. "What are you trying to do, land us all in a war?" she yelled at the hunters.

"Throw down your guns at once. Show the squirrels that we do not mean to hurt them. According to reports, they are civilized creatures and peaceful at heart. Perhaps they can be persuaded to turn around and go home."

Civilized creatures? The hunters gaped at her. Turn around and go home? Even Amber had to admit it was impossible now. The masses of squirrels closing in on all sides looked utterly barbaric. Their small, fierce bodies filled the branches overhead. Their snapping heads swirled across the forest floor. They trampled bushes in their path and surged through the trees in thick gray rivers. Gradually, as their hordes converged, the squirrels formed a living wall around the terrified group. Then the rustling stopped, and Amber felt the weight of alien eyes upon her.

Without another word from Chief Teckstar, the hunters dropped to one knee and raised their guns to their shoulders. They sighted down their barrels and put their fingers on the triggers. Wendell dropped to one knee, too. He drew his slingshot from his back pocket and tucked a stone in the sling.

"Well, I guess this is it," he rasped to Amber, who sat down suddenly on the ground beside him. With a wild gesture, half of anger, half of despair, she buried her face in her hands. Behind her, Professor Spark clenched her fists, and for a long minute all of Forest seemed to hang in some dreadful, final balance.

Then an odd ripple of movement passed through the squirrels in the trees. Low chitters erupted, and the swarms on the ground swayed and began to break apart. Like a series of veils drawn aside, the ground squirrels parted, and a wide channel opened between them.

"What is happening?" Chief Teckstar whispered. The answer soon appeared.

"It's the troop of silver-haired squirrels!" exclaimed Amber, who had raised her head to look. "See? They're coming toward us." Nearby, she heard her father murmur in surprise. Professor Spark stood speechless, her mouth dropped open.

The strange raft of bodies advanced slowly, but with such precision that there was no sign of the many legs working beneath. Like a cloud, the silver squirrels floated out from the mass of others and came to rest in the space between the squirrels and the humans. As the hunters nervously fingered their guns, the silver squirrels raised their heads. From their throats came the wonderful chitter and whir that Amber and Wendell had heard before.

"Listen! They're speaking to us!" Amber said, leaning forward in delight.

"What are they saying?" Mr. Padgett asked.

"I'm not sure," she replied. "I can almost hear it, but . . ." She listened with all her might to the soaring voices. "I know there's a pattern, but I can't quite hear . . .

"Wait a minute!" shouted Amber. "Yes, I can! *Stop,* they're saying! The silver squirrels are telling us to stop."

"Stop what?" Chief Teckstar said. "We haven't done anything."

In the next moment the squirrels' raft began to turn slowly around. The elegant gray heads turned also, until they were gazing at the squirrel hordes crowding in on all sides. Then, low and high, their voices soared again, soft and loud, quick and slow.

"Stop!" whispered Amber. She looked at Professor Spark.

"They are telling the squirrels to stop. They say the fight is pointless and everyone must go home."

"Amber Padgett, are you making this all up?" demanded her father. "I can't hear anything but a lot of chitters and squeaks."

"Amber never makes anything up!" Wendell said, stepping up to his father fiercely. "Don't you know anything about her by now?"

There was no time for a reply. The silver squirrels fell suddenly silent, and there rose, as if in answer, ten thousand chitters and ten thousand deep-chested whirs from the huge congregation of squirrels all around. Never had anyone in the group heard such a noise before. The sound was thunderous— but gentle.

"Like wind blowing through a canyon," Mr. Padgett tried to explain to Mrs. Padgett later. "Or a crowd of people saying a prayer."

"And then what happened?" Mrs. Padgett asked.

And then, well, how could Mr. Padgett describe what he'd seen? How could Chief Teckstar or any of them? It was unbelievable. One moment the tree limbs swarmed with squirrels; the next, they were empty. One moment a massive gray army surrounded them with deadly eyes; the next, it had melted away. And only the silver-haired squirrels remained behind, twitching their tails in a strangely intelligent way. It was enough to make you wonder if the varmints had minds.

Amber and Wendell had seen something even more extraordinary, however. It was something that kept them wondering for a long time after about what really happened that day in the squirrels' treetop world. . . . As the gray armies disappeared, they caught sight of three small squirrels crouched to one side of the silver-hairs' raft.

"Wendell, look! Doesn't that look like . . ."

"It is! It's our little squirrel. I'd recognize her anywhere. And guess who's sitting beside her."

"The one-eared squirrel who came to rescue her. And the other one, his pretty friend."

"But are they silver-hairs, too?" Wendell asked. "They're sitting with them as if they were."

"I don't know," Amber said. "They look too young. Do you think they had anything to do with all this?"

"I bet they did," said Wendell. "Though exactly what we'll probably never figure out."

"I don't know why not," said Professor Spark, interrupting just then. "It's the very sort of thing I would like to look into. And now that Amber has cracked the squirrels' language code . . ." The tiny woman winked at Amber while Wendell grinned at them both.

"Well, ahem," said Amber. "I suppose that was going a little far. I didn't really know what the silver-hairs were saying. I was just so afraid that the hunters would start shooting."

"It was an excellent translation, to my mind," the professor said dryly. "And made in the nick of time. Which brings me to my point: would either of you be willing to start a research project on these squirrels with me? I believe, after today's amazing events, I can have them placed on the endangered species list. Not that they are any more endangered than we are, you understand. (I have an idea that humans may be the ones in real trouble.) But it will keep certain people in Forest from going on with the war."

At this they all glanced over to Mr. Padgett, who, to give him credit, didn't appear very angry. He seemed, in fact, rather awed by what he'd seen.

"And the incredible thing is, these squirrels have probably been here all along!" he could be heard exclaiming to Chief Teckstar. "It's just that no one ever bothered to look up before."

"Professor Spark," said Amber, "I'd love to do research with you. And with India," she added, nodding respectfully at the frightful dog, who had come to join her mistress in the crowd of hunters. "I still think these squirrels are peaceful at heart."

"Well, I think they're a bunch of maniacs," Wendell said to the professor. "From what I've seen, they're exactly like humans, only worse. But if Amber is studying them . . ." He turned to his sister. "Amber, are you sure you want to go back up in these trees?"

"Oh, I do!" she said, waving her broken arm. "As soon as I get this cast off, it's the one thing I want to do!"

"Well, then I'll go with you," Wendell said bravely. "How else am I supposed to figure anything out? Mom and Dad never tell me anything."

"Come on!" cried Amber. "Let's get moving. We have to let the town of Forest know it's been saved."

"I'm right behind you!" called Professor Spark. "Though India wants her dinner, I see, and may take a quick trip into the forest to get it. Never pass up a chance for fresh meat, as they say. . . . Go ahead, cutie pie. You can catch us later," she assured the dog, while Amber backed away in alarm.

"Um . . . Wendell," said his father, swinging into step beside him. "I've been noticing your new interest in the forest.

Hiking around, sleeping out, adventure in the wilds—just the sort of thing a boy your age should be doing. I wonder if you might like a tent for your birthday?"

"A tent! Are you kidding? I'm never sleeping outside again!" shouted Wendell. "Even Amber can't make me do that. I'm keeping a roof over my head from now on. And I'm never going hunting again with you, either, Dad. So don't ask."

Mr. Padgett shook his head as Wendell ran ahead to catch up with his sister. "You know, I really don't understand children," he muttered. "They're like people from another planet. We just don't speak the same language."

·UPPER·FOREST·

"Well, there they go," said Woodbine, watching the aliens' long-stemmed shapes begin to move away into the forest. "I never thought we'd get out of this alive."

"Whew! Me either," Brown Nut replied. "The Elders are extraordinary leaders. I've never heard them speak with such wisdom and humbleness. They took the blame for everything, though everyone knows how willingly the squirrels turned to cruelty and war. The whole of Forest is in shock over it. If the Elders hadn't woken up and recalled us to our ancient ways, what then?"

"What else," Laurel replied, "but Barkers and more Barkers. We shall have to be careful in the future."

"What will happen to Barker, anyway?" Woodbine asked.

"I believe the Elders have ordered him to leave Forest," Brown Nut said. "He must never return to the end of his days."

"And is that so terrible?"

Brown Nut flicked her tail at her brother. "Oh yes, I remember. You are the one who wants to move to the sea. But think, Woodbine, what good would it do if you could never come back to tell us what you saw?"

"Oh, I would come back," Woodbine said quickly. "There's never been any question about that."

"Look!" Laurel interrupted. "There is the invader herself. And her brother."

"Where! I can't believe they are here," Woodbine exclaimed. "See? In the middle there."

"Don't look now, they are staring straight at us!" Brown Nut chittered.

Woodbine gave a tremendous sigh and inched forward on the ground. "Such a fascinating creature," he murmured. "I wonder . . . if I put off my travels for a while, would either of you be interested in doing a study with me? Of the invader, I mean, and her strange Lower Region? Who knows, we might learn something."

"Certainly not!" screeched Brown Nut. "We've had enough trouble with that place already. I am getting down to work. What with all this business of battles and troops, we are far behind in our food-gathering schedule. Really, Woodbine, you are the worst sort of goof-off."

"I would be interested," Laurel said quietly, after a pause.

"You would?"

"Yes. Shall we set up a headquarters in the blackberry bush by the pond?"

"Immediately!" cried Woodbine. "What a wonderful idea!"

Leaving Brown Nut behind to sniff at their behavior, the two mink-tails spiraled happily up a trunk and vanished into the branchways of Forest's majestic trees.

Janet Taylor Lisle is the author of many other novels for middle readers, including the Newbery Honor Book *Afternoon of the Elves*, *The Great Dimpole Oak*, and *The Lost Flower Children*. She lives on the coast of Rhode Island with her husband and their daughter, Elizabeth.

Visit her Web site at **www.JanetTaylorLisle.com**.